"What about the military? Didn't they do anything for the holidays?"

He paused by the front door. His back went ramrod-straight.

"I always opted to be on duty," he said, his tone clipped.

"You're home now. Time to start over. A chance for new beginnings…" Her voice trailed off. She didn't want him to misconstrue her words—to think she wanted *them* to have a new beginning. "You should try joining in the fun. After all, it's the most joyous time of the year."

Kara forced a smile. She couldn't believe she was trying to talk him into celebrating the exact same holiday in which he'd broken her heart. If he wanted to be an old, cranky Scrooge, why should she care?

Jason didn't say anything as he opened the door and stepped aside, allowing her to enter. In the narrow opening her arm brushed against him, and even through the layers of clothing an electrical current zinged up her arm, warming a spot in her chest.

Staying here wasn't a good idea.

Being alone with her new boss was an even poorer idea.

This whole situation constituted the worst idea…ever.

Dear Reader

I'm thrilled to be able to share this holiday romance with you. It's a story of love and forgiveness...of facing down one's deepest fears in order to find peace and acceptance. My fondest hope is that this story will touch you as deeply as it did me.

Do you remember the youthful rush of falling in love? The undeniable certainty that you'd found 'The One'? Well, Kara and Jason were those young lovers with stars in their eyes...until their fairytale suddenly veered into a nightmare.

Now, seven years later, a lot has changed...especially Jason—a returning war hero with jagged scars that run deep. But Kara has changed as well. No longer is she a naïve young girl. She has tremendous responsibilities weighing on her and no time to waste on what-might-have-been. However, when old flames are reignited will the Ghost of Christmas Past destroy any chance of a future? Or will they learn the true depths of forgiveness and its power to open doors to a new beginning?

I really rooted for these two, having laughed and cried with them. They're two wounded people who refuse to give up until they've earned their happily-ever-after, and in the process bring a smile to my heart.

Happy reading!

Jennifer

SNOWBOUND WITH THE SOLDIER

BY
JENNIFER FAYE

MILLS & BOON

First published in Great Britain 2013
by Mills & Boon, an imprint of Harlequin (UK) Limited.
Harlequin (UK) Limited, Eton House, 18-24 Paradise Road,
Richmond, Surrey TW9 1SR

© Jennifer F. Stroka 2013

ISBN: 978 0 263 23564 7

Harlequin (UK) policy is to use papers that are natural, renewable and recyclable products and made from wood grown in sustainable forests. The logging and manufacturing process conform to the legal environmental regulations of the country of origin.

Printed and bound in Great Britain
by CPI Antony Rowe, Chippenham, Wiltshire

In another life, **Jennifer Faye** was a statistician. She still has a love for numbers, formulas and spreadsheets, but when she was presented with the opportunity to follow her lifelong passion and spend her days writing and pursuing her dream of becoming a Mills & Boon® author, she couldn't pass it up. These days, when she's not writing, Jennifer enjoys reading, fine needlework, quilting, tweeting and cheering on the Pittsburgh Penguins. She lives in Pennsylvania with her amazingly patient husband, two remarkably talented daughters and their two very spoiled fur babies otherwise known as cats—but *shh*…don't tell them they're not human!

Jennifer loves to hear from readers—you can contact her via her website: **www.JenniferFaye.com**

A recent book by Jennifer Faye:

RANCHER TO THE RESCUE

Did you know this is also available as an eBook?
Visit www.millsandboon.co.uk

This book is dedicated to the real life Sly. A beautiful, sweet black cat who crossed my path and stole my heart. She was my muse for this heart-touching story.

Sly, you passed through our lives far too quickly. You are missed.

CHAPTER ONE

OLD MAN WINTER huffed and puffed, rattling the doors of the Greene Summit Resort. Kara Jameson turned her back on the dark, blustery night. She didn't relish heading out into the declining weather to navigate her way home after a very long day at work.

She took a moment to admire the massive evergreen standing in the lobby of what had once been one of Pennsylvania's premier ski destinations. The twinkling white lights combined with the sparkling green and red decorations would normally fill her with holiday cheer, but not tonight. Not even the rendition of "Jingle Bells" playing softly in the background could tempt her to hum along.

The resort had been sold. The somber thought weighed heavily on her shoulders. It didn't help that rumors were running rampant that all the management positions were being replaced. Why did it have to happen with Christmas only a few weeks away?

Everything will work out. Everything will work out. She repeated the mantra over and over in her mind, anxious to believe the old adage. But something in her gut said nothing would ever be the same again.

"Kara?"

The deep baritone voice came from behind her. She froze. Her gaze remained locked on a red bell-shaped ornament as her mind processed the sound. Even in the two syllables of her name, she knew that voice, knew the way her name rolled off his tongue as sweet as candy.

Jason Smith.

It couldn't be. He'd sworn he would never come back.

"Kara, won't you even look at me?"

Her gaze shifted to the glass doors that led to the parking lot. Her feet refused to cooperate, remaining cemented to the swirled golden pattern on the hotel carpet. Seven years ago, she'd bolted out those exact doors after Jason had broken their engagement. Back then she'd been unsure and confused by the depth of her emotions. Since then life had given her a crash course in growing up. Running was no longer her style.

She sucked in a deep breath, leveled her shoulders and turned.

Clear blue eyes stared back at her. A slow, easy grin lifted the tired lines around Jason's eyes. She blinked, but he was still there.

This couldn't be happening. The overtime and lack of sleep must be catching up with her.

"Are you okay?" He reached out to her.

She jumped back before he could touch her. Words rushed up her throat, but clogged in her mouth. She pressed her lips together and willed her heart to slow. Her pulse pounded in her ears as her fists clenched at her sides. A breath in. A breath out.

"You're so pale. Sit down." He gestured to one of the overstuffed couches surrounding the stone fireplace. "You look like you've seen a ghost."

She didn't move. This surreal moment struck her as a clip from a movie—a visit from the ghost of Christmas past. Only, this wasn't a Hollywood soundstage and he wasn't an actor.

She studied the man before her, trying to make sense of things. The dark scruff obscuring his boyish features was a new addition, as was the two-inch scar trailing up the right side of his jaw. His hardened appearance was a visual reminder of the military life he'd chosen over her. Her fingers longed to reach out and trace the uneven skin of his jaw, but instead she gripped the strap of her tote even tighter. A bit older and a little scuffed up, but it was most definitely Jason.

Just pretend he's a mere acquaintance from years ago, not the man who threw your love back in your face and walked away without any explanation.

"Jason Smith. I can't believe you're here," she said, trying her best to sound casual.

"Actually, I go by Jason Greene these days...."

The fact he now used his mother's maiden name came as a surprise, but Kara supposed she shouldn't find it too shocking, knowing the stormy relationship between him and his father. The name change had presumably contributed to her inability to track him down and notify him of his father's failing health. A question teetered on her tongue, but she clamped her lips shut. Playing catch-up with Jason was akin to striking a match near fireworks. One wrong move and it'd blow up in her face. Best to stick to safe topics.

His gaze implored her for an answer, but to what? She'd lost track of the strained conversation. "What did you say?"

"How are you?"

He wanted to exchange pleasantries as though they'd parted on good terms? She didn't have time to beat around the bush. She should already be home, getting dinner for her daughter before they went over her homework.

"When you left Pleasant Valley, you swore you'd never

return. So what happened? What finally changed your mind?"

His expression hardened. If he'd been expecting a warm welcome, he'd been sadly mistaken.

He shrugged. "Things change."

Well, most things did, and generally not for the better, but not in Jason's case. He hadn't gained so much as a beer gut or a receding hairline. Even the jagged scar on his face added to his sexiness.

Kara's gaze rose to meet his. At first glance, she thought his intense blue eyes were the same as she remembered, but a closer inspection revealed a hard glint in them. He no longer resembled the warm, lighthearted guy she'd dated for nearly four years. Or had he been that way all along? Had those rose-colored glasses she'd been wearing back then obscured his real character? Had she ever truly known him at all?

Jason hitched his thumbs in his jeans pockets. "I'm sorry about what happened between us. I handled it poorly."

"You certainly did."

"If I could explain, I would, but I can't—"

"Don't." She held up a hand, stalling his too little, too late explanation. "Nothing you say will change what happened."

Her pride refused to let on that his presence affected her, that even after all this time she longed to know what had changed his mind about marrying her. She reconciled herself to the fact that she was better off not knowing—not prying open that door to her past.

Jason shifted his weight from one foot to the other. "I guess it was too much to hope that you'd be willing to put the past behind us."

She lifted her chin, drawing on the strength she'd used

to manage this place in the recent absence of her boss, who also happened to be Jason's father. "I've moved on."

It'd taken time—lots of time—but she'd gotten over him and the way her life had unraveled after he'd dumped her. She refused to let him get under her skin again. Besides, she had enough on her plate already.

After working her way up through the ranks, to now be dismissed from her hard-earned position would be utterly demoralizing. She'd like to think she was needlessly worrying, but the rumors said the new owners wanted their own people running the show—people with more education and experience.

She went to step around Jason, but he snagged hold of her arm. "Wait. I need to apologize."

Even through her coat she could feel his warmth radiating into her body. She yanked at her arm, to no avail.

"Let go," she said with a hard edge. He couldn't just worm his way past her defenses with an empty apology. She refused to let him off the hook that easily. "If you were truly sorry, you'd have said something before now. You wouldn't have ignored me all these years or returned your father's letters unopened."

His hand slipped from her arm. "You know about that?"

She tightened her hold on the strap of the tote bag slung over her shoulder, which held the red scarf she was knitting for Jason's father for Christmas. "Yes. He told me. After you left, he was never quite the same. Not knowing if you were dead or alive seemed to age him overnight."

Jason's body visibly stiffened. "I think you've mixed my father up with someone who cares."

"He's sick, Jason. Real sick. I've done what I can to help him, but he needs you."

"I don't want to discuss him."

She should turn away and walk out the door before the

snow grew any deeper, but her feet wouldn't cooperate. There was one thing she needed to know—one nagging question that demanded an answer.

She licked her dry lips. "If it isn't because of your father, then why have you suddenly returned home?"

"Do you really care?" His gaze never left hers.

"No. Never mind. I shouldn't have asked."

Her pulse quickened. Heat scorched her cheeks. Even though it was a lie, she refused to let him think that she cared anything about what he said or did. He was part of her past...nothing more.

"I have to go." She needed space to make sense of things.

"Kara, I know we can't go back to the way things used to be, but it doesn't have to be this awkward. We were friends for years before we dated."

They had been the best of friends. She'd told him everything about her life, but apparently that openness had been one-sided. She wouldn't make the mistake of trusting him again.

"Does this plea of friendship mean you're planning to stay in Pleasant Valley?"

"Yes."

The blunt response lacked any telling details of what had prompted his unexpected return. Her errant gaze strayed to his bare ring finger. Still single. Still available. Been there, done that. She glanced away.

"Welcome home." She buttoned her black peacoat. "I really do need to go."

"Be careful. The snow's picking up." His gaze moved to the glass doors. "It looks bad out. You should spend the night at the hotel."

She shook her head. "The resort's closed for renovations. You shouldn't even be here. Who's been showing you around?"

They weren't the only ones there late. With the new owner, GSR Inc., arriving on Monday, a number of people were working late even though it was a Friday evening. Everyone had gone above and beyond their duties, hoping to make a good impression on the new owner. Though Jason had been away for years, a number of employees knew him and would have volunteered to give him a last look around the place.

She glanced up at him, waiting for a response. His lips were pursed as though he was about to say something, but had refrained.

"I don't have all night," she stated.

"I don't need an escort."

Kara squared her shoulders. "Since I'm in charge around here, I'm telling you that either you have an escort or you must leave. Now."

This close to the new owner's arrival, she wasn't taking any chances. The last thing she needed was for anyone to get hurt on her watch.

Jason's brows arched. "You like being the boss, don't you?"

"I do whatever needs to be done to keep this place going."

"Good. I hope all my employees are so devoted."

"Your employees…?" Alarm tightened her throat, smothering her next words. Surely she hadn't heard him correctly. Or she'd misunderstood.

"Yes, my employees."

This nightmare couldn't be unfolding right before her eyes. "You…you're GSR?"

"I've gone in with a couple of investors. This place needs to be reorganized. A lot of cutting needs to be done, but I think it's possible to turn the business around with the right management."

A lot of cutting? Right management? The implication of his words shattered her dream of keeping her job. Fragments of her hopes scattered over the freshly laid carpet. Finding an equivalent job would not be easy without a college degree. She inwardly groaned.

She might even have to move. Her thoughts turned to her parents, who had been involved in their only grandchild's life since the day she was born. To tear her daughter away from them now would devastate not only them but her little girl, as well. But Kara wouldn't have a choice. She would have to move wherever she could find reasonable employment.

"Time to start job hunting," she muttered under her breath.

"What?"

"Nothing. I have to go before the snow gets too deep to drive in." She yanked on her gloves. "Good night."

Kara forced herself to take measured steps, training her gaze on the glass door. She hadn't run away when the locals had clucked their tongues and shaken their heads at her youthful mistake. Now she wouldn't give Jason the satisfaction of witnessing how he could still shake her to the core.

Jason Greene clenched his hands. He'd heard enough of her mumbled comment to know she had no intention of working for him. He couldn't leave things like this. Her assistance and knowledge over these next several weeks were essential to the resort's success. He'd risked everything he owned on restoring the Greene Summit. And he couldn't afford to lose it all now.

He started for the door. Large snowflakes fell, adding to the several inches of accumulation on the ground. He'd forgotten how fast the weather could deteriorate in the Laurel Highlands. An overwhelming urge settled in his chest to stop her and convince her to stay over in one of the hotel rooms, where she'd be safe and warm during this stormy night.

His steps grew quicker. Damn, he still cared about her. This was bigger than when they'd grown up together—back when Kara was 100 percent tomboy and he'd protected her from the school bully. The emotions brewing inside him now had an adult edge.

He lingered at the glass doors, staring out into the stormy night. He couldn't tear his gaze from Kara's petite figure as she braved fierce winds while crossing the snowy parking lot. Her appearance had changed, from jeans and snug T-shirts that nestled against her soft curves, to casual business attire. A short haircut replaced her ponytail. Everything combined to give her a mature, polished persona. He certainly wasn't the only one who'd changed.

Was she worried about her trip home? Or was she doing the same as him and reliving the past? He still had time to stop her. He pushed the door open. The bitter wind stung his face as he followed her footsteps. She would demand once more to know the sordid details behind his seven-year absence. His pace slowed. Could he bring himself to explain that dreadful night?

He stopped. No. No way. If he knew the words to make everything right between them, he'd have said them years ago. As the cold cut through his coat and over his exposed skin, he realized he'd played out all the scenarios in his mind thousands of times. Each ended with her looking at him with repulsion. No way could he put either of them through that experience.

Jason rubbed the back of his neck, trying to ease the

stiff muscles. His return to the Summit was going to be just as rough and bumpy as he'd imagined, but he'd get through it. He turned and limped back to the lobby. Only one day on his feet, with the cold seeping into his bones, and already the wound in his thigh throbbed.

He exhaled a weary sigh. The last time he'd worked at the resort, Kara had been his priority. Now, with no significant other in his life, he could sink his dreams into restoring this place without all the emotional entanglements of a relationship and raging teenage hormones. His experience in the military had forced him to grow up. He now realized what was important and why.

He shoved his fingers through his hair, hating the selfish boy he'd once been. This time he'd prove himself worthy of the trust others placed in him. He wouldn't repeat the mistakes of his past.

Muffled footsteps drew his attention. He glanced over his shoulder to find his childhood friend Robert Heinze approaching him. He looked every bit the professional in his navy suit, and definitely fit the part of a distinguished attorney.

"Jason, what are you still doing here?"

"While I was walking the grounds, I came across some maintenance men working on a problem with the towrope for the bunny hill."

"And from the grease stains on your jacket and jeans, I'm assuming you couldn't just let the staff handle it on their own."

Jason shook his head. "I'm not good at standing around watching when I could pitch in and lend a hand."

"You'll have plenty of time to play Mr. Fix-it after tomorrow. By the way, I heard the roads are getting bad. If you don't leave now, you might find yourself riding out the storm right here."

"Before I go, I want to thank you for finalizing this sale with my father. Without you going back and forth between us, I don't think an agreement would have ever been reached."

Robert flashed a small smile. "I think you give me too much credit. You were the mastermind behind this whole venture. I hope it turns out the way you planned."

"It will." He'd returned a couple of days ago, and until the deal had become official, he'd intentionally kept a low profile. "By the way, I just ran into Kara Jameson."

He didn't know why he'd mentioned it. Maybe he just wanted someone to talk some sense into him. After all, before Robert had moved away to be an attorney in downtown Pittsburgh, he'd grown up right here with Kara and Jason.

"Did you tell her you bought this place?"

He nodded.

Robert shrugged on his coat. "How'd it go?"

"The news took her by surprise."

"Seems like an understandable reaction. You've been gone for years." His old friend paused and looked intently at him. "What else is bothering you? Did she quit on the spot?"

"Not exactly."

"Then why do you look like you just chugged a carton of sour milk?"

"Kara lit into me about ignoring my father. He must have fed her some kind of lies to gain her sympathy." Jason didn't bother to hide the loathing he felt.

Robert let out a low whistle. "Boy, you didn't exaggerate about the rift between you two."

If anything, he'd understated the distance between himself and his father. Every muscle in Jason's body grew rigid at the thought of their insurmountable differences. He refused to dwell on something that could never be fixed.

With the help of a couple of investors, he'd at last gained ownership of his heritage—the resort his grandfather had founded. His gaze moved around the lobby, taking in its splendor.

"I've thought of nothing else for the past year but of making this place mine, of restoring the Greene Summit back to its former glory, like when my grandfather was alive. I'll make him proud. No matter what it takes."

Robert patted him on the shoulder. "Then you might want to start by being honest with Kara. I've talked with her and she's bright. When your father's health started to decline, he leaned on her to keep this place running. By now, she must know where each and every skeleton is buried. You're going to need her."

"I know. I'll tell her everything Monday." Well, not everything—just the parts pertaining to the Greene Summit.

Robert's brow furrowed and he began patting his pockets. "I must have left my phone in the office. I'll run back and grab it."

"Okay. I'll see you in the morning."

"Get some sleep. We've got work to do."

Jason turned to the lobby doors and gazed out at the parking lot. He rubbed his thigh, trying to ease the persistent throbbing. He had a business to rebuild and no time to slow down.

The grand reopening in three weeks had to go off without a hitch. All his investors would be on hand to take part in the festivities, and their approval was of the utmost importance, especially if he wanted more capital to undo the years of neglect.

He knew he could never again be the man in Kara's life.

Still, he had to find a way to get her to stay on at the resort. He needed her knowledge to make this a smooth transition.

But when she preferred braving a snowstorm to staying safe here with him, how in the world would they be able to work side by side?

CHAPTER TWO

THE HYPNOTIC SWIRL of flakes made it difficult for Kara to focus on the winding mountain road. The cascade of snow hit the windshield harder and faster with each passing minute. She flicked on the wipers. The built-up ice on the rubber blades made an awful ruckus. *Swish. Thunk. Swish. Thunk.*

The knowledge that Jason was now her boss haunted her. She'd thought that, with the resort sold, any lingering ties to him would be severed. How could she have been so wrong?

A bend in the road loomed ahead. Her foot tapped the brake a little too hard and the car lost traction. Her fingers tightened on the steering wheel as she started to skid.

Stay calm. You know how to drive in this weather.

Thoughts of Jason vanished as she turned into the skid. Like a pinball shot into action, the vehicle slid forward. Trees and the guardrail whizzed by in a blur. In an attempt to straighten the car, she spun the wheel in the other direction. Her throat constricted. At last, she came to a stop in what she hoped was the middle of the road.

That was way too close.

The pent-up air whooshed from her burning lungs. She

rested her forehead against the steering wheel, trying to calm the frantic thumping of her heart. She silently sent up a thankful prayer.

On her way to work that morning, the radio announcer had mentioned the possibility of light snow flurries this evening but never alluded to a foot of snow. And it still continued to fall.

She let off the brake and crept forward, anxious to put as much distance between herself and Jason as possible. Would she ever be able to sweep away the tangled web of attraction, woven tightly with strands of resentment? She sure hoped so, because as long as she lived around here, they were bound to run into each other. After all this time, she'd expected to feel absolutely nothing where he was concerned. So why did she let him get to her?

She exhaled a frustrated groan and glanced down to crank up the heater. When she looked up again, a brief flash caught her attention. Her gaze focused off to the side of the road, where her headlights reflected off a pair of eyes staring back at her. A millisecond later, a deer darted into her path.

A screech of terror tore from Kara's throat as she tramped the brakes, braced for the inevitable collision. Like a skater on a sheet of ice, the car careened over the slick pavement. At the last second, the deer jumped over the hood, just as the front tires dropped off the pavement.

Kara's foothold on the brake slipped, sending the car off the road. She pitched forward, but the seat belt jerked her back, slamming her into the door. With a thud, her head careened into the driver's side window. Pain splintered through her skull. The sound of ripping metal pierced the inky darkness.

At last the car shuddered to a halt. The air bag thumped hard into her chest, sending the breath whooshing from her lungs. She clung to the memory of her daughter's sweet smile.

With newly attached chains on the SUV's tires, Jason drove cautiously down the curvy mountain road. Soon he'd be home, enjoying a piping-hot bowl of leftover stew. His stomach rumbled in anticipation.

He stared out the windshield at the dark, desolate road. When he was a kid, there would have been a string of headlights passing him as anxious skiers flocked to the resort to try out the fresh snow. Tonight, the only evidence of another soul on this road was the faint outline of tire tracks.

Was it possible they belonged to Kara?

The thought of making peace with his childhood sweetheart weighed heavily on his mind. He didn't blame her for still being angry with him. She had every right to be furious over the way he'd walked out on their engagement. He'd probably act the same way if their roles had been reversed. No, he'd have been worse—much worse.

If only there was a way to make her understand that even though he'd handled it poorly, his leaving had been the only answer. But he had no idea how to convey that to her without going into the details of that fateful night, and that was not something he was willing to do. Not even to save the Summit, his birthright.

The wipers were beginning to lose their battle with the thickening snow. He turned on the vehicle's fog lamps, hoping they'd give him a better idea where he was on the road.

The tire tracks he'd been following suddenly veered to the right. His stomach muscles tightened. Trying to get a rescue squad out for an accident during this storm would take hours. He'd best go investigate first. He gently applied pressure to the brakes. The tires fought for traction, sliding a few yards before the SUV stopped. He glanced around, not spotting anyone standing next to the road. Not a good sign. They could be injured or worse.

He grabbed a flashlight from the glove compartment and flicked the switch, sending a light beam out the window. He squinted, trying to see through the thickening snow. At last he spotted the tracks. They led off the road into a gulley. Concern sliced through him. *Please don't let it be Kara.*

He threw the SUV into Park, switched on the flashers and jumped out. Wet snow tossed about by the biting wind stung his face. If Kara was out here, he'd find her.

With his hand shielding his eyes, he marched forward. Piercing pain shot down his thigh as he forced his way through a drift. He gritted his teeth and kept moving. From the edge of the road, he shone the light down at what appeared to be a ten-foot drop. At the bottom was a car with its front end smashed against a tree trunk. Whoever was in it was in need of help.

He'd just started down the embankment when his foot slipped. Hot pain shot through his knee and up his thigh, and his eyes smarted as he choked back a string of curses. Beads of perspiration ran down the sides of his face. But he couldn't stop now. He had a mission to complete.

His fingers curled around a branch and, using his good leg, he regained his balance and sucked in an unsteady breath. He massaged his knee, hoping he hadn't just undone the surgeon's long hours of reconstructive surgery, and weeks of physical therapy. Cautiously Jason flexed the joint. A new wave of agony swept up his body and socked him in the gut. It might hurt like the dickens, but it still worked. That had to be a good sign.

When he reached the two-door coupe, he tapped on a snow-covered window. "I'm here to help. Open up."

The window inched down, letting the buildup of flurries spill inside. Jason flashed his light into the dark interior. A hand immediately shot up, shielding the occupant's eyes from the glare.

"Jason?"

"Kara?" He leaned down, trying to see her better. "Are you all right?"

"I don't know. I think so." Her breathy voice held an eerie squeak. "There was a deer. Then the car skidded off the road. The door's stuck and my phone won't work."

"Okay, slow down. First thing we've got to do is get you out of there."

She started pushing on the door with her palms. He tried pulling on the handle. Without warning, she slammed her shoulder into the door. A grunt followed, but she pulled back, ready to repeat the process.

"Stop!" He used his drill sergeant voice, hoping to gain her attention. "Sit still."

"But I smell gas."

The mention of a gas leak shot a dagger of fear through his chest. Jason surveyed the area with the help of the flashlight, soon spotting the reason the door was stuck. The bottom was jammed against the embankment. The passenger door was pressed against a tree trunk.

"I need out!"

"Wind down your window the whole way."

"It's stuck." Her eyes grew round as her palms pressed against the glass. Her fingertips slipped through the opening and curled over the edge. "Help me."

The frigid wind continued to throw snow through the opening. With these low temperatures, he needed to get her out—fast. He kicked the ground, hoping to find a rock beneath the white blanket of frozen moisture.

At last, armed with a decent-size rock, he used his drill sergeant voice again. "I've got to break the window to get you out. Turn away. And cover your head with your coat."

She did as he instructed, and soon he was assisting her through the opening. When her foot sank down into the deep snow, she lost her balance and pitched to the side. He caught her, hugging her slight form to him. Her hands clutched at his shoulders, pulling him closer. When her head came to rest on his chest, he breathed in the faint scent of strawberries. The feel of her body next to his and the enchanting smell of her all came together, jumbling his senses.

Unable to resist the temptation, he ran his fingers over her golden locks. "It's okay," he murmured. "You're safe now."

Her weight shifted fully against him. Warmth filled his chest. After all those long, lonely nights in different towns and countries, Jason felt as if he'd finally found his way home. He never wanted to let her go.

A gust of wind threw wet snow in his face, bringing him back to his senses. He shouldn't be holding her. It was wrong to enjoy their closeness. He'd sacrificed that liberty years ago. And he was no longer the same man she'd once known.

He held her at arm's length. "You're bleeding."

"I am? I don't feel a thing."

He cupped her face in his hands. A crimson streak trailed from her forehead to her cheek. *Please don't let it be serious.*

"Are you sure? No headache? No double vision?"

"Nothing."

Ever so gently he wiped away the blood with his thumb.

When he found only a minor cut, he breathed a little easier. "Tell me if you start to feel bad."

She nodded.

He pulled his phone from his pocket, punched in the numbers for help and held the device to his ear. After a few seconds, he moved, positioning the phone in front of him. "I can't get a signal. Looks like we're on our own."

She shivered, wrapping her arms around her midsection. "How will I get my car out of there?"

He gave her a quick once-over. Aside from the small cut, he didn't see any other signs of trauma. "The car's not going anywhere tonight. And if you smelled gas, we aren't taking any chances. The tow truck people can deal with it tomorrow."

Her body shook and her teeth chattered. "Now…what… am I going to do?"

He worried about shock settling in. He was certain the accident had been horrific enough, but then to be trapped, even for a brief time, might have been too much for her.

"My SUV's up on the road. We need to get you warm."

He ushered her up the short embankment to his vehicle, which still had the engine running. After she climbed in, he reached behind the seat and pulled out a blanket. "This should warm you up."

He was about to close the door when she said, "Wait. I need my stuff from the car."

She started to climb back out, but he placed a hand on her shoulder, holding her in place. "I'll get your stuff. You wait here and turn up the heater."

"My purse is there…in the backseat…and my cell phone."

Jason closed the door and yanked his gloves from his pocket. He hobbled along, doing his best not to stumble on the uneven ground. The coldness seemed to freeze all but one of his thoughts: *Kara.* He'd missed her much more than he'd been willing to admit to himself. Between her pouty lips and soulful eyes, it was tempting to forget the demons that lurked in his past.

But that couldn't happen. He couldn't let himself go soft in the brain. It wouldn't be fair to her. Soon they'd be off this mountain, he assured himself. Once he gathered her belongings from the car, his only agenda was to deliver her safely to her doorstep and leave.

He limped to the wrecked vehicle and ran the flashlight's beam from trunk to hood. A sour taste rose in the back of his throat. In the military he'd witnessed the tangled metal wrecks and human carnage caused by IEDs, so this accident scene shouldn't evoke a reaction—certainly nothing like the wave of nausea washing over him. But he couldn't escape the fact that Kara could have died here tonight.

He blocked the awful thought from his mind. She was safe, he assured himself. All he had to do now was retrieve her belongings and drive her home.

Long minutes ticked by before Jason reappeared in the glow of the headlights. *Thank goodness he's back.* Soon she'd be home, snug and warm, with her family. Still, something struck her as not quite right. She gazed through the window, giving him a second, more intense inspection. She noticed he moved with a limp. The knowledge that he'd been hurt while rescuing her gave her pause.

When he yanked the back door open, she asked, "Are you all right?"

"I'm fine."

After placing her belongings on the backseat, he closed the door with a loud thud and climbed in beside her. It'd been a long time since they'd been together, but as close as they were physically, they'd never been so far apart in every other way. And it would remain that way. It was for the best.

But that didn't mean she could ignore his physical pain. "You aren't fine. You were limping."

"Don't worry. I'll be fine after I rest my leg for a bit."

The lines etched around his eyes and mouth said the pain was more severe than he'd admitted. Once again he was holding back the truth.

"Can I do anything—for your leg?"

He shook his head. "The, uh, weather—it's getting worse. We better get moving. Are you ready?"

"Definitely. I'm anxious to get home. I don't want my family to worry."

He yanked off his snow-covered hat and tossed it in the backseat. When he unbuttoned his coat, a fluff of pink fur poked out. Kara gaped at him. Nothing about him either in the past or now screamed pink fuzzy anything.

He withdrew the object. "I found this on the floor in back when I was searching for your purse."

"Bubbles." Her daughter must have forgotten the stuffed animal that morning, when Kara had dropped Samantha off at her grandparents' house before school.

"Huh?" Jason's gaze darted from the teddy bear with Baby Girl embroidered on its belly to her. "Bubbles? Really?"

Kara reached for the stuffed animal. "Something wrong with the name?"

"Uh…no." He tossed her the ball of fluff. "Not at all."

"Hey, it's the color of bubble gum—hence the name Bubbles."

"Logical. I guess."

She glanced at him, expecting to find humor easing the tense lines marring his face, but his expression hadn't changed. What had happened to the old Jason, the one with a thousand and one fast comebacks and an easy grin? Sadness burrowed into her chest. She mourned the boy who had always made a point of making her smile, even during the worst teenage crisis.

She hugged Bubbles to her chest. "Thanks for rescuing him."

"The bear is really yours?" Suspicion laced every syllable. "You carry a baby's toy around in your car?"

She stared down at the bear. It had been her daughter's very first stuffed animal. Even though Samantha had accumulated an army of plush toys over the years, she still reached for Bubbles when she was tired or upset.

Kara considered pretending she hadn't heard the question. However, she recalled how Jason had been worse than a hound dog rooting around for a bone when he wanted information. He would continue to hunt and dig until he found exactly what he was after.

Maybe a glib answer would suffice. She did know one thing: she certainly wasn't prepared to blurt out the entire truth about her daughter. So she'd give him the basics, and hopefully, he wouldn't ask any more questions.

"The bear belongs to my daughter."

CHAPTER THREE

SERIOUSLY, COULD THIS night get any worse?

Kara didn't say anything more, hoping he'd get the hint that she didn't want to talk. Her daughter was off-limits to him. She turned her head and stared out at the starless night, which mirrored her dismal mood.

"So you're a mother?"

The astonishment in his voice set her on edge. This was the very last topic she wanted to discuss with him. After all, she didn't owe him any explanations. She didn't owe him a single thing. Her daughter was no secret, but that didn't mean she had to share the circumstances of her birth with him.

"A lot changed after you left."

"Obviously. So who's the lucky man in your life?"

Kara suddenly hated her single status. The thought of lying tiptoed across her mind, but she'd never been any good at it, even as a kid. Best to stick with the truth. "There is no man."

"Thought you'd have guys lined up, waiting to take you out."

"And you'd be wrong."

She smothered a sigh. After he'd dumped her and she'd found out she was pregnant, it was a very long time until she was willing to trust any man. When she finally did dip her toe in the dating pool, finding a man with the right personality, who was ready to take on a young mother, was a challenge. Most of the guys she met simply didn't want the hassle of a ready-made family. And they certainly weren't thrilled about having their social calendars dictated by whether or not Kara could secure a babysitter.

Not that she'd become a nun or anything. She'd dated here and there. The evenings out were nice, but that's all they were—nice. She shielded her daughter from her dating life. She didn't want Samantha getting attached to someone, only to lose him when things didn't work out.

Sensing Jason giving her periodic glances, Kara refused to meet his gaze. Instead, she continued to stare into the night. The thickening snow kept her from spotting the pond where they used to skate as kids. In those days, they'd been practically inseparable. Did Jason ever think about the good old days? Did he even regret his abrupt departure from her life and this community? Was that why he'd finally come home? To make amends?

She sneaked a glance at him. His long fingers clenched the steering wheel, fighting to keep the vehicle on the road. When he turned his head to glance at her, she jerked her gaze away, focusing on the hypnotic swish, swish of the windshield wipers.

A loud crack echoed through the night as a tree limb fell onto the road. "Watch out!"

He cut the wheel to the left. The driver's side tires dropped off the snow-covered pavement. Kara's upper body jerked to the left, where firm muscles pillowed her and held her steady. Jason's body was rock hard. The kid she'd planned to explore the world with was long gone, and in his place was this man she barely recognized. The army life had transformed him into a human tank. And in that moment, she knew he'd protect her.

Thankfully, the vehicle slowed to a stop. With some effort, Jason eased it back on the road. "Sorry about that. You okay?"

Realizing she was still leaning against his arm, she pulled herself upright. "I'm fine."

But was she? Her heart continued to palpitate faster than a jackhammer. The blood pounded in her ears. It was the near miss with the tree limb that had her all riled up. She was certain of it. She settled back in her seat and took a calming breath.

"Hang on tight." Jason released the brake and the vehicle crawled forward. "The weather's getting worse. I can barely make out the road."

The tires crunched over the snow blanketing the pavement. The wind created white sheets that draped over the vehicle. All the while, the wipers worked furiously to clear the windshield for a second or two at a time. How in the world was she going to get home tonight? It'd be dawn before they got down the mountain at this inchworm pace.

"What are we going to do?" She didn't bother to hide the quaver in her voice.

Jason patted her leg. "We'll be okay. Trust me."

He was the very last person she should trust, but in these extreme circumstances, she didn't have much choice. Heat emanated from his lingering touch and radiated outward, sweeping through her limbs. Her gaze zeroed in on his fingers gripping her thigh. She should pull away, at the very least shove his hand aside. Before she could act, he withdrew it himself, to grip the steering wheel.

"Kara, why are you still there—at the resort? Working for my father?"

Not exactly a subject she wanted to broach with him, but at least it kept him from asking about her daughter. "You mean why didn't I leave him like you did?"

"That isn't what I meant." A note of bitterness wove through his tone. "Why haven't you moved on with your life? Gotten away from here? You always dreamed of traveling the world. Why give it all up for an old drunk who ran my grandfather's dream into the ground?"

She straightened. "Don't you dare judge me. Your father and I did our best to keep the resort up and running. Maybe if you'd been here, you could have helped."

"I was busy at the time, getting shot at while defending our country." He turned to her, his eyes glittering. "And recovering from a bomb blast."

Her brain stuttered, trying to imagine the dangers he'd faced. "I had no idea."

"You weren't supposed to. I shouldn't have mentioned it."

"What happened? Are you okay now?"

"I'm fine."

"If you're so fine, why are you here and not still overseas?"

A muscle flexed in his cheek. "They gave me a medical discharge."

She realized abruptly that something awful had happened to him. For all she knew, he might have come close to dying. A shiver washed over her body. Common sense said she should let the subject drop. After all, he was no longer part of her life, and she couldn't afford to let him back in.

But the tense silence set her frazzled nerves on edge. Maybe some light conversation would ease her anxiety about the weather. "Your father must be so relieved to know you're home. That you're safe."

"I haven't seen him. And I don't know if I will."

Shocked at his admission, she paused. It wasn't right that these two men, who had only each other, should be so distant. She fiddled with the blanket's satin binding while staring out at the storm. Time was running out for his father. She felt compelled to try to help them.

"You have to go to him," she insisted. "His liver is failing. I tried to put him on the transplant list, but with his history, he isn't a candidate."

"You can't expect me to act surprised. No one can drink at breakfast, lunch and dinner without paying for it in the end."

"Jason!" She glared at him.

In all the time she'd known him, he'd had a strained relationship with his father. Kara surmised it had started with the death of Jason's mother, but none of that explained why Jason had turned his back on his dad after so many years. She couldn't imagine ever cutting herself off from her parents. They didn't have a perfect relationship, but her folks were always there when she needed them, and vice versa.

Refusing to believe Jason could be so cold, she said, "The next time I stop by the nursing home, I'll let him know you're in town."

"Don't interfere. That man and I took care of everything we had to say to each other years ago. There's nothing left between us."

Jason's rigid tone told her she was pushing her luck, but she couldn't help herself. "But he's changed. He's sober—"

"No more." Jason's hand slashed through the air, as though drawing an imaginary line she shouldn't cross. "I can't argue with you. I need to focus on the road."

She sagged back against the seat with a heavy sigh. He was right. Now wasn't the time to delve into the situation with his father. At best, Jason would be only partially listening to her while he worked to keep them out of a ditch. At least she'd had a chance to make her point about his father's condition. There wasn't much more she could do now. She just hoped Jason would come to his senses and make peace with his dad before it was too late. Regrets were tough to live with. She should know.

She reached for the radio, then paused. "Do you mind if I turn on some music?"

"Go ahead."

At the press of a button, an ad for a local grocery store resonated from the SUV's speakers. Kara turned the dial, searching for her favorite country station. The headline news greeted her. She glanced at the clock on the dash. With it being the top of the hour, news would be on most every station.

"This bulletin is just in from the National Weather Service," the radio announcer said in a somber tone, garnering Kara's full attention. "The arctic express is supposed to dump twenty-four inches of snow in the higher elevations by tomorrow."

"Two feet," she said in horror.

"We'll be okay." Jason reached over and gave her hand a reassuring squeeze. An army of goose bumps marched up her limbs. She assured herself it was just a reaction to the dire forecast and had nothing to do with his touch.

The radio crackled as the announcer's voice continued to ring out. "That isn't even the worst of the storm. Sometime this evening, a blast from the south will raise the temperature, only to have the thermometer quickly sink back below freezing. I know you're thinking this is a good thing, but let me tell you, folks, those pretty little flakes are going to change into an ice shower, and with a wind advisory due to kick in at midnight, it's going to get dicey, resulting in downed trees and power lines…."

After another advertisement, strains of "Let It Snow" began to play. Someone at the radio station had a sick sense of humor. Outside, the flakes were continuing to come down hard and fast. A glance at Jason's squinted eyes and the determined set of his jaw told Kara the conditions were already beyond dicey.

Minutes later, when the vehicle skidded to a stop next to an old elm tree, outside a modest log home, she turned to him. "What are we doing here?"

"The roads are too dangerous. We'll hunker down here until the storm passes."

"Here?" A half-dozen snow-covered trees surrounded them. "In the middle of nowhere?"

"This isn't the boonies. There's heat and shelter. You'll be fine. Trust me."

There he went again with that line about trust. The words grated across her thinly stretched nerves. What in the world had she done for Fate to conspire against her?

"I can't spend the night with you," she protested, even though she knew her daughter would be safe with her parents.

Jason leveled a frown at her, as though he wasn't any more pleased than she was about the situation. "You aren't scared of being alone with me, are you?"

"Don't flatter yourself," she said a little too quickly, refusing to meet his intense stare. "I grew up a long time ago."

Her lips pressed into a firm line as she surveyed the sprawling log structure. Being snowed in with Jason, of all people, would be more stressful than sliding down the slick mountain road. Her hands clenched. She and Jason had too much history, and she hated how he still got under her skin, evoking a physical awareness she hadn't experienced in ages.

"Do you even know who lives here? Or are we about to commit an act of breaking and entering?"

"This is now my home. Don't you remember it? I

brought you here a couple of times to visit my grandmother."

Her gaze moved past him to the covered porch, with its two wooden rocking chairs. She searched her memory. At last she grasped on to a vague recollection that brought a smile to her lips. "I remember now. She fed us chocolate chip cookies fresh from the oven. I liked her a lot."

"She liked you, too." His lips quirked as though he'd been transported back in time—back to a life that wasn't so complicated. "I inherited this place from my grandparents, along with a trust fund my father couldn't squander."

Glowing light from the dashboard illuminated Jason's face, highlighting the discomfort he felt when mentioning his dad, as he opened the door, letting the frigid air rush in. "Wait here. I'll leave the heat on while I shovel a path to the porch."

She refused to let him overexert his injured leg again on her behalf. With a twist of the key, she turned off the engine and vaulted out of the SUV. She sidled up next to him as he limped along.

He frowned down at her. "Don't you ever listen?"

"Only when I want to. Now, lean on me and take some pressure off your leg."

He breathed out an exasperated sigh before draping his arm over her shoulder. She started to lean in closer, but then pulled back, keeping a respectable distance while still assisting him. She refused to give in to her body's desire to once again feel his heat, his strength. She had to keep herself in check. This was simply a matter of he'd helped her and now she was returning the favor—that was all.

On the top step, they paused. Her eyes scanned the lengthy porch. Her gaze stopped when she noticed a freshly cut pine tree, all ready to be decked out in colorful ornaments and tinsel. She remembered as a child accompanying her father and grandfather to the local Christmas-tree farm to cut down their own tree. The fond memory left her smiling.

"I'm so jealous," she said as Jason pulled away to stand on his own. "You have a real Christmas tree. All I ever have time for is the artificial kind. I remember how the live trees would bring such a wonderful scent to the whole house."

"A neighbor asked to cut down a tree on my property, and thanked me by chopping one for me, too. The thing is, I don't do Christmas."

"What do you mean, you don't do Christmas?" Her eyes opened wide. "How do you not do Christmas? It's the best time of the year."

"Not for me." His definite tone left no doubt that he wanted nothing to do with the holiday.

Her thoughts strayed to her daughter and how her eyes lit up when they put up the Christmas tree. Even in the lean years before her promotion to office manager, Kara had managed to collect dollar-store ornaments and strings of lights. With carols playing in the background, they would sing as they hooked the decorations over the branches.

The holiday was a time for family, for togetherness. A time to be grateful for life's many blessings. Not a time to be alone with nothing but your memories for company. The thought of Jason detached from his family and friends during such a festive time filled her with such sorrow.

"I haven't celebrated it since…my mother was alive." His last words were barely audible.

Kara recalled when they were dating how he'd always have a small gift for her, including the silver locket at home in her jewelry box. But he'd always made one excuse after another to avoid the Christmas festivities.

"Surely after all these years you've enjoyed Christmas

carols around a bonfire, driven around to check out the houses all decked out in lights or exchanged presents with various girlfriends?" Kara didn't want to dwell on that last uneasy thought.

He shook his head.

"What about the military? Didn't they do anything for the holidays?"

He paused by the front door. His back went ramrod straight.

"I always opted to be on duty," he said, his tone clipped. "I'll get rid of the tree the first chance I get."

"How could you possibly throw away such a perfect tree? You're home now. Time to start over. A chance for new beginnings..." Her voice trailed off. She didn't want him to misconstrue her words—to think she wanted them to have a new beginning. Not giving him time to ponder her statement, she continued, "You should try joining in the fun. After all, it's the most joyous time of the year."

Kara forced a smile. She couldn't believe she was trying to talk him into celebrating the exact same holiday during which he'd broken her heart. If he wanted to be an old, cranky Scrooge, why should she care?

Jason didn't say anything as he opened the door and stepped aside, allowing her to enter. In the narrow opening, her arm brushed against him, and even through the layers of clothing an electrical current zinged up her arm, warming a spot in her chest.

Staying here wasn't a good idea.

Being alone with her new boss was an even poorer idea.

This whole situation constituted the worst idea ever.

CHAPTER FOUR

ALARM BELLS CLANGED loud and clear in Kara's mind.

There had to be a realistic alternative to staying, but for the life of her, she couldn't come up with anything reasonable. One hesitant step after another led her across the threshold and into the log house. Warmth enveloped her in an instant.

"It's getting really bad out there." Jason slammed the door against the gusting wind before stomping the caked snow from his boots. "Let me get some lights on in here."

He moved past her to a table and switched on a small antique lamp with little blue flowers painted around the base. The soft glow added warmth to her unfamiliar surroundings.

"Thanks." She clasped her shivering hands, rubbing her fingers together.

When her eyes adjusted to the lighting, her curious gaze meandered around the place Jason called home. Worn yet well-kept maple furniture stood prominently in the room, with a braided, blue oval rug covering a large portion of the oak floor. Nothing flashy, but not dingy, either—more like cozy and comfortable.

Jason favored his leg as he made his way to the fireplace and arranged some kindling. He struck a match, and soon a golden glow gave his hunched figure a larger-than-life appearance. What would it be like to curl up with him on that leather couch with a hot mug of tea and a fire crackling in the stone-and-mortar fireplace? To sit there and discuss the day, or make plans for the future?

She gave herself a mental shake. This wasn't a romantic vacation. Nor was she interested in curling up with him now or ever. She'd keep out of his way and wait out the storm. Once the weather broke and the plows cleared the roads, she'd be gone. And it couldn't be soon enough.

She tugged her soggy jacket tighter, trying to ward off the chill that went clear through to her bones. All the while, she continued to examine her surroundings. A wadded up pile of white sheets lay on one of the armchairs, as though Jason was still in the process of making himself at home. Her attention moved to the oak coffee table with a folded newspaper and a tidy stack of what appeared to be sports magazines.

"Something wrong?" he asked.

"You mean other than being snowed in here with you?" She couldn't resist the jab. She didn't want either one of them to get too comfortable in this arrangement and forget about all the problems between them. "Actually, I'm surprised to find this place so clean. I guess I just don't think of men as being neat freaks. Unless, of course, you're living with someone…."

The thought hadn't occurred to her until then, and it annoyed her that it even made a difference to her. Yet the presence of a girlfriend would assure their past remained in the hazy shadows, along with the snarled web of emotions.

"I'm not involved with anyone." The flat statement left no doubt in her mind about the status of his bachelorhood. "I learned to clean up after myself in the military. You've got to be prepared to move out on a moment's notice, and you can't be ready if your gear is in a jumbled heap."

The tension in Kara's stomach eased. Instead of examining her worrisome response to finding out he had no one special in his life, she chose to stick to safer topics.

Glancing up, she said, "I love the cathedral ceiling and how the chimney rises into the rafters."

"Wait until you see this place with the morning sun coming in through the wall of windows on the other side of the room."

Preferring not to dwell on the idea of watching the sunrise with him by her side, she pointed past the fireplace. "What's over there?"

"My grandfather used the area as a study, and I didn't feel a need to change things."

She glanced around, taking in the winding stairs. "Where do those go?"

"To the loft. When I was little my grandparents used it as a bedroom for me. I'd spend hours up there playing. Now the space is crammed full of junk. Maybe this summer I'll get around to throwing it all out."

"Why would you want to do that? There are probably heirlooms up there that you'll one day want to hand down to your children."

His thick brows puckered. Storm clouds raced across his sky-blue eyes. "One man's treasure is another man's junk. And since I'm not having kids, I don't need the stuff."

Not having kids. The knowledge knocked the air from her lungs. He made it sound so final, as though he'd already given the subject considerable thought. She'd never heard him say such things when they'd been dating. In fact, they'd discussed having a boy and a girl. A little Jason and a little Kara.

In that instant, she realized a stranger faced her. *What could have changed him so drastically?* She bit back the question. None of her business, she reminded herself.

Dredging up these old memories stung worse than pouring rubbing alcohol over a festering wound. Her judgment concerning men seemed to be made up of one painful mistake after another.

"I'll get us something warm to drink," he said, ending the conversation. "You can get out of those wet clothes in there." He pointed to a door on the opposite end of the great room.

"I don't have anything to change into. Besides, I need to call my family."

"You need to get warmed up before you come down with pneumonia. Then you can phone home. It's not late, so they shouldn't be too worried yet."

She hoped he was right.

When Jason bent over to untie his boots, he groaned in pain. She grabbed his arm, tugging him upright. He started to pull away, but she tightened her grip, noticing how his muscles rippled beneath her fingertips. In spite of her awareness of his very muscular build, she dragged him over to a wooden chair beneath the picture window.

"Sit," she commanded, in the same tone she used when Samantha was being uncooperative. "You don't need to put any more pressure on your sore leg."

His startled gaze met hers. Then, ignoring her words, he once again attempted to loosen his laces. She swiped his hand away.

"I'll do it," she insisted, kneeling before him.

Her cold fingers ached as she dug her short nails through the chunks of ice, trying to loosen the laces.

"So this take-charge woman you've become, is it part of being a mother?" he asked, startling her with the intimate question.

"I suppose so." The mention of her daughter, combined with his nearness, flustered her. Her fingers refused to cooperate. "I almost have your boots untied. There's just this one knot…".

She bit down on her lip, forcing her attention to remain on the frozen tangle and to ignore how easy it'd be to end up in his capable arms. With one last pull, followed by a solid yank, she loosened the laces. And none too soon. This proximity was short-circuiting her thought processes.

She jumped to her feet and strode over to the fireplace. Why did this log home have to be so small? She supposed *small* wasn't a fair description, as this all-purpose room was quite spacious. But it didn't allow for any privacy, any breathing space away from Jason.

Her gaze shot to the two doorways off to the side, below the loft. Maybe she could wait out the storm in one of those rooms.

"I'll find you something to wear." Jason got to his feet. "Come on."

He led her to the nearest bedroom. Before he even opened the door, she guessed it was his. Definitely not her first choice for accommodations. She couldn't imagine sleeping in his bed, surrounded by his things.

"What's in the other room?"

"Wall-to-wall furniture. My grandmother had the great room loaded with so much stuff you could hardly get around."

So much for that great idea.

She stepped into his room. It wasn't spacious, but roomy enough for a dresser and a double bed. Her gaze lingered on the bright colored scrap quilt covering the mattress. The thought of being here alone with Jason had her lingering at the doorway.

Her mind reeled back to the summer of her sophomore year in college. Jason had told her that he wanted to leave Pleasant Valley, that he was joining the army. In the very next breath, he'd proposed to her. He wanted to elope with her after she earned her journalism degree. The answer had been a no-brainer—a very definite "Yes!" But she hadn't wanted to wait. She'd planned to drop out of college and earn her degree via the internet while following Jason around the world. She'd been so certain she could make it work.

She recalled how they'd made love over and over, celebrating their impending nuptials. At the time, she'd thought her heart would burst from the abundance of love. Never once had they been bold enough to come together in the luxury of a bed. Their special spot had been a remote pasture near a creek at the back of the resort, where the warm rays of the sun had kissed their bodies. The place hadn't been important, only that they were alone to talk, laugh and love each other.

When Jason abruptly left Pleasant Valley—left *her*— seeing the world was no longer an option. As the only child of two loving parents who worked manual labor jobs to get by, Kara realized as soon as she learned she was pregnant that she couldn't burden them with another mouth to feed. The day after she'd finished her junior year of college, her job at the Greene Summit Resort went from part-time to full-time.

Youthful endeavors and girlish dreams were lost to her. With the most sweet, well-behaved baby counting on her, Kara grew up overnight. Her parents were supportive, but the bulk of the responsibility for child care fell to her, whether she'd been up half the night for feedings or exhausted from a strenuous day at work. It was a lot to adjust to, but she would do anything for her daughter— then and now.

The dresser drawer banged closed, jarring her back to the here and now. When Jason handed over a pair of gray sweatpants and a flannel shirt, their fingers briefly touched, causing her heart to skip a beat.

"Thank you." She jerked her hand away.

"The bathroom is just through that door." He pointed over his shoulder. "I'll go get you something warm to drink."

"You should rest your leg," she protested.

"I'm fine. But you won't be if you don't get out of those wet things."

Before she could utter a rebuttal, the door thudded shut. Irritation niggled at her. Did that man always have to have the last word?

She rushed over to the door, only to find it lacked a lock. Nothing like feeling utterly vulnerable. With a sigh, she turned and leaned back against the door. She stood there for countless minutes with his clothes clutched to her pounding chest. She inhaled deeply and Jason's manly scent assailed her senses. She couldn't resist burying her face in the soft flannel. Even though it had obviously been laundered, spicy aftershave clung to the material. He wore the same brand as he had years ago. Okay, so maybe not everything about him had changed. She smothered a groan of desire.

After everything that had happened, why did she still have a weakness for him? But no matter how many memories bombarded her, they couldn't go backward. What was broken between them couldn't be undone. The only thing for them to do now was to take a step forward—in opposite directions.

Determined to stave off her lingering attraction to him, she rushed off to the bathroom. The pulsating water eased her achy muscles and the billowing steam soothed her anxiety. She refused to let the crush of memories overwhelm her. She just had to treat Jason in the same gracious manner she would anyone else who rescued her.

Minutes later, dressed in the warm clothing, she glanced in the oval mirror mounted above the chest of drawers. Kara didn't need to inspect her reflection to know she looked ridiculous, as though she'd just fallen out of a Salvation Army donation bin. She cinched the baggy sweats around her waist so they didn't slip down over her hips, and rolled up the dangling sleeves.

That left dealing with her hair, which was an absolute mess. She attempted to finger-comb the waves, but it didn't help. Surely there had to be a brush or comb around here. She scanned the dresser top, taking in the papers and envelopes haphazardly dropped in the middle. She noticed how there were no photos of people from his past or ones currently in his life. It was as if he was a clean slate just waiting to be written on, but she knew that was far from the truth.

A small, flat box sticking out from beneath the papers snagged her attention. Though she knew it was none of her business, a longing to learn more about this man from her past had her reaching for the box. It creaked open. Suspended from a red-white-and-blue ribbon was a gold five-point star with a laurel wreath surrounding a silver star in the center. Her heart swelled with pride for Jason. Her eyes grew moist as she realized he must have put his life on the line to receive such a great honor.

With her thumb, she lifted the medal and read the engraving on the back: For Gallantry in Action. A tear dripped onto her cheek. Jason was a bona fide hero. Just not *her* hero.

A brief knock at the door drew her attention. "Uh… coming."

She repositioned the medal and snapped the lid closed.

Just as she was about to return the box to its original spot, the door squeaked open.

Heat swirled in her chest before rushing to her cheeks and ears. Nothing like getting caught red-handed, snooping. Still, part of her was glad she'd learned this important detail of Jason's life. Knowing their country had taken time to recognize him for risking his life touched her deeply. Before her stood a rock-solid hero with broad shoulders, hefty biceps and a chest any woman would crave to be held against—except her.

Kara refused to let his gallant acts or obvious good looks change what she knew about him. When a relationship got too serious or hit a snag, he'd rather skip town than talk out their problems. She refused to get involved with someone she couldn't trust.

His blank stare moved from the box in her hand to her eyes. "I have the water heated up. I just need to know if you want tea or coffee."

"Tea." Her mouth grew dry and she struggled to swallow. Giving herself a moment to suck down her embarrassment, she took her time returning the box to the dresser top. At last she turned. "I didn't read about your heroism in the paper."

He leaned against the doorjamb and crossed his arms. His eyes needled her. "Snooping, huh?"

She didn't know if her face could get any hotter without catching fire. Unable to deny his accusation, she went with a different tack. "Such a great honor shouldn't be kept a secret."

"And that justifies you going through my things? Digging up unwanted memories?" The roughness of his voice spoke of a deep emotional attachment to the memories.

"Why were you honored?" she asked, needing to understand what had happened to him during those missing seven years.

"I did what had to be done. End of story."

"Does everything have to be some sort of deep dark secret? Or is it just me that you refuse to be honest with?"

Pain reflected in his eyes, but in a blink, it was gone—hidden behind an impenetrable wall. Regret for snapping at him rolled over Kara. She hadn't meant to make him defensive. She truly cared about what had happened to him.

"I'll get you some tea."

"You don't need to bother." She didn't want to be even more of an imposition. "I can just wait in here, out of the way, until the snowplow digs us out."

"I don't think that's a good idea."

"It's for the best. This way we don't have to get in each other's way. You can go about your business like I'm not even here."

"This room isn't very warm. You'll be a lot more comfortable in front of the fireplace."

"I could just bundle up in a blanket."

Why was he being so difficult when she was trying to make this awkward arrangement as tolerable as possible for both of them? Surely he wasn't any more interested in spending time with her than she was about spending it with him.

"Suit yourself." He shrugged. "But you should know that as soon as I get your tea, I'll be in to get my shower. And with the bathroom being a bit cramped, I tend to strip down in the bedroom."

Heat scorched her cheeks until she thought for sure her hair would go up in smoke. So much for her idea about keeping distance between them.

"I'll be out in a minute," she said. "You wouldn't have a comb handy, would you?"

He pulled one out of his rear pocket and tossed it to her before walking away.

She turned back to the dresser, catching sight of the box containing his medal. She hated that he refused to open up to her. But he wasn't the only one keeping secrets. She had things in her past that she preferred not to discuss—especially not with him. Maybe he was right. Nothing good would come of them opening up to each other.

After doing what she could with her hair, she walked into the living room to find the fireplace crackling with a decent-size blaze. The glow of the burgeoning flames filled the room with dancing shadows.

A movement on one of the chairs drew her attention. A black cat stood and stretched, arching its back. Kara stepped forward. The cat poised at the edge of the chair, ready to scamper away.

"It's okay. I won't hurt you."

The cat sent her a wide-eyed stare, as though trying to make up its mind about her. Finding her not to be an immediate threat, it sat down.

"Well, aren't you a cutie? I'm surprised you'd live here with Mr. Scrooge. You know, he wasn't always so grouchy."

Kara glanced around, making sure they were alone. A clank followed by a thud assured her Jason was still in the kitchen. Now would be a good time to contact her family.

"I'll be back," she told the cat, whose golden eyes followed her every movement.

With her outerwear wet, Kara borrowed Jason's far-too-large boots and a dry blue coat that was hanging on a wooden peg by the door. She rushed out into the driving snow to retrieve her belongings from the SUV. She hoped and prayed her cell phone hadn't been damaged in the accident. Once back on the covered porch, she dropped her stuff on one of the rockers. A quick search of her tote revealed her phone had survived the accident. The lights twinkled across the screen and displayed a weak signal. It'd have to do.

Her parents would be anxious to hear from her. She always called when she was going to be late, and she refused to take advantage of their generosity. Only tonight, there was no way she was going to make it home. She hit the speed dial and pressed the cold plastic to her ear.

Crackle. Crackle. Ring.

By the fourth ring, she began to worry. Surely her parents hadn't done anything foolish, like heading out in this storm to hunt for her. She paced back and forth. *Please let them be safe.*

As though in answer to her prayer, her father's voice came over the line. "Kara? Is that you?"

"It's me, Dad."

Crackle. "…been so worried."

"Dad? I can hardly hear you."

"Kara…" *Crackle.* "…and Samantha are all right. Where are you?"

"I'm at the resort." The answer was close enough to the truth without having to get into the sticky explanation about spending the night with her ex-fiancé. "The roads are impassable. I'll be home tomorrow."

"Okay, be…"

Crackle. Crackle. Silence.

Time to deal with Jason. What in the world would they discuss? Her mind raced as she rushed back inside to warm herself by the fire. There had to be some sort of casual conversation they could make to keep the tense silence at bay.

The weather? A mere glance outside pretty much summed up that depressing subject.

The resort? It was bad enough being snowed in with

the new owner. If firing her was part of his reorganization plan, she didn't want to find out tonight.

The past? The mere thought soured her stomach. That subject was best left alone.

Perhaps in this case silence truly was golden.

Jason reached into the far corner of the cabinet above the stove. Luckily, a neighbor had presented him with a welcome basket containing some tea bags. Not knowing what to do with them, he'd stashed the bags in the back of the cabinet. He never imagined he'd be serving Kara, of all people, some chai tea.

His mind was still reeling from the news that she was now a mother. As he placed the mug of tea on an old tray, an image of her with a baby in her arms filled his mind. Uneasiness settled in his gut. Years ago, when he'd proposed marriage, he'd been too young to think much about kids, other than someday they'd have two. A boy and a girl.

Even though he'd wanted her to move on, he'd never thought he'd be around to see her again. And he'd certainly never imagined she'd end up a single mom. A fiery rage slithered through his veins and burned in the pit of his stomach. The guy who'd abandoned Kara and her little girl better hope Jason never crossed his path.

Jason opened the fridge, removed a jug of milk and banged it down on the counter. What excuse did this man have for walking away from Kara? Sure, he himself had done the same thing, but there hadn't been a baby involved. He'd left in order to protect Kara from what he'd learned about himself. At the time, he'd been in shock, and repulsed by the ugly words his drunken father had spewed at him. Emotionally wounded and in trauma, he'd needed to get away from everyone he knew, including Kara.

The memory of the tears streaking down her cheeks,

dripping onto her new green Christmas dress, still bowled him over with self-loathing. His jaw clenched. He'd totally botched the entire situation. Now he deserved her contempt, and anything else she could throw at him. He was a mature man, a soldier, he could shoulder her wrath. Besides, she couldn't say anything about him that he hadn't thought at some point.

"Do you need any help?" she called out from the other room.

"I'll be right there."

He gathered his thoughts while retrieving a big bag of sugar from the cabinet. With everything balanced on the tray, he headed back to the living room, expecting to find Kara on the couch, snuggled under one of his grandmother's quilts. When he found the cushions empty, he paused.

"Hey, sweetie," Kara's soothing voice called out.

The tray rattled in his hands. Sweetie? Every nerve ending stood on high alert. Had he heard her correctly?

"Come on over here," she crooned.

His heart careened into his ribs with enough velocity to leave a big bruise. Where was she? In the bedroom? A flood of testosterone roared through Jason's eager body, drowning out the pleading strains of his common sense.

"Hey, big boy. You know you want to. I promise I won't bite."

CHAPTER FIVE

JASON SNAPPED HIS gaping mouth closed. His jaw clenched, grinding his back teeth together.

The tray in his hands tilted. The tea sloshed over the rim of the cup, while the sack of sugar slid to the edge. He righted the tray before the contents could spill onto the floor. In haste, he safely deposited the armload on the table.

"Kara?" He cleared the hoarseness from his voice. "Where are you?"

"Over here."

He scanned the couch and the two easy chairs, but saw no sign of her. "Quit playing games."

"I'm down here."

His gaze fell to the floor, and in the corner, behind the easy chair, he spotted the most enticing derriere sticking up in the air.

"Come on, sweetie," she coaxed. "A little closer."

His heart rate shot into the triple digits and showed no signs of slowing down. He reached for the back of the couch to anchor himself. His ears must be playing tricks on him. She despised him…didn't she?

"Please," she crooned. "I promise to be gentle."

"Kara," he said. "What are you doing?"

"There's the sweetest kitty under this chair."

"You're talking to the cat?"

She raised her head to look at him. Amusement danced in her green eyes. "You thought I was talking to you?"

Her lips bowed and a peal of laughter danced through the room, making him all the more uncomfortable.

"It's not funny!" The air grew uncomfortably warm and he yanked at his shirt collar. He shouldn't have built that fire up so much. "Leave the cat alone. She'll come out if she wants to. Your tea's on the table. I'm going to grab a shower."

He headed for the bedroom, needing a cold, cold shower to set him straight. On second thought, he'd be better off to go outside and roll around in the mounting snow. He could just imagine the steam billowing off his body. How was it possible that woman could still drive him crazy, like some hormonal teenager?

With the door firmly closed, he raked his fingers through his hair. He sucked in a ragged breath. The cat. He shook his head in disbelief. Wow, he'd been alone way too long.

Maybe once he got the resort back in operation, he'd consider spending an evening or two with a cute snow bunny. The problem was when he closed his eyes and sought out the ideal woman to spend time with, his mind automatically conjured up Kara's image.

Jason groaned. Boy, he was in deep trouble. If he couldn't keep his feelings for her in check for this one evening, how in the world would they work together?

Kara got to her feet, giving up on her attempts to befriend the cat, for now. Still chilled, she grabbed the red-white-and-blue patriotic quilt from the back of the couch and draped it over her shoulders. She made her way to the scarred oak table, where her now lukewarm tea waited.

A smile pulled at her lips as she thought of Jason preparing her tea.

She pulled out one of the ladder-back chairs and made herself comfortable. The table was strategically placed in the room, giving the occupants somewhere to dine while admiring the landscape, which at this moment was hidden beneath a fluffy white blanket of snow. Coldness radiated through the windowpanes, sending goose bumps cascading down her arms. She clutched the quilt tighter.

Some hot tea would help warm her up. She dug a teaspoon into the five-pound sack of sugar and ladled out three even spoonfuls. All the while, her mind replayed the moment when Jason thought she'd been calling out to him and not the cat. She couldn't help but notice the flame of desire that had burned in his eyes. Knowing he was still interested in her unfurled a ribbon of excitement within her. Long-ignored needs swept over her, making her weak in the knees.

The spoon clanked against the mug a little too hard, jarring her attention back to stirring the tea without making a mess. They weren't meant to be, she reminded herself. She'd learned that unforgettable lesson the hard way. She didn't need a repeat. Someday she'd find the right man. He was out there somewhere.

Still, she was intrigued to know that beneath Jason's grouchy, war-hardened veneer was a kind, caring heart— one capable of opening up his home to a stray cat and an old love. She thought of mentioning her observation to him—but what was she thinking? She needed to stop dwelling on her sexy host. But being stuck with him in this cozy log home, she had no way to avoid him.

What she needed to do was keep herself busy. But doing what? She couldn't remember the last time she'd been faced with having to find something to occupy her time. Usually there weren't enough hours in the day, to help Samantha with her homework, do the laundry, cook dinner...the list went on and on. But here in Jason's home, Kara felt out of sorts.

She had just lifted the warm mug to her lips to savor that first sip of tea, which was always infinitely better than the rest, when Jason entered the room with his hair still damp from the shower. His scowl was firmly in place. In fact, the only time he'd appeared the slightest bit at ease was when he'd thought she was flirting with him. *Not going there,* she reminded herself.

"When did you get a cat?"

"I didn't."

She glanced across the room, finding the aforementioned feline sitting on the coffee table. Kara couldn't help but smile as the sleek feline let out a big yawn, showing off its pink tongue. "Are you going to try to tell me there isn't a black cat sitting across the room, staring at us?"

His forehead creased. "Of course there's a cat. But I didn't get her. She just made herself at home."

"So it's a girl. And let me guess, she was hungry and you started feeding her."

He shrugged a shoulder. "Something like that."

So the curmudgeon wasn't as hard-hearted as he wanted to let on. "What's her name?"

"Sly."

A kitty with a name was a kitty with a permanent home. "Sly? Hmm...what kind of a name is that for a girl cat?"

"For a person with a stuffed bear named Bubbles, I wouldn't be casting any stones."

Kara, feeling childish, stuck her tongue out at him. His blue eyes grew round and his pupils dilated. All the blood swirled in her chest and rushed up her neck. Obviously, that wasn't the right move to make around a man who'd just moments ago thought she was flirting with him. She inwardly groaned, wondering if she'd ever figure out how to act around him.

"Do you think Sly will ever let me pet her?"

"The way to make nice with that cat is through her stomach. If you feed her, you'll be friends for life."

Kara paused at the mention of friends for life. She wouldn't be around after tonight. In fact, she had no idea where she'd be this time next year, after Jason replaced her at the resort. Not that she intended to give him any reason to fire her. When she left she wanted it to be on her terms—with a stable job waiting, to support her and her daughter.

"How about I fix us some food?" she asked, anxious to do something—anything.

"Dinner's already taken care of," he said, getting to his feet while keeping his gaze averted. "You'll have to make do with leftover stew."

If he was anticipating an argument, he wouldn't get one. "Sounds good. Anything I can do to help?"

"No, it only needs to be warmed. Shouldn't be long. Then you can feed Sly. She eats when I eat. Keeps her occupied so she isn't stealing my food."

Kara laughed, trying to imagine such an innocent-looking thief. "Just call if you need me."

Of course he wouldn't *need* her. He'd made that abundantly clear seven years ago.

His plan was working. He'd made it through that conversation like a true host. No errant thoughts or overtly awkward moments. He just had to keep his cool a bit longer.

With the bread buttered and the stew ladled into bowls, Jason returned to the living room. He couldn't help but notice how Kara looked at home. Her hair was in disarray, and her cheeks were rosy, as though they'd just spent a lazy afternoon making love. His gaze drifted downward, catching sight of his plaid shirt with just enough buttons undone that when she leaned toward the cat he caught a glimpse of her lacy white bra. His mouth grew dry.

In some distant part of his brain, Jason knew he shouldn't be staring, but the sight was too delicious to turn away. He never would have imagined that old flannel shirt could look sexy on anyone, but he doubted Kara could look bad in anything.

Every muscle in his body grew rigid and he swallowed hard. This wasn't right. She shouldn't be here. It would be way too easy to slip back into an old, comfortable routine with her. His gaze continued to drink in her beauty, impressing it upon his memory, because that was as much of her as he'd allow himself.

When she cleared her throat and straightened her top, his gaze jerked upward, meeting her jade-green eyes. He resisted the urge to tug on the collar of his T-shirt to let out the steam coming off his heated body.

"Here, take this," he said, his voice gruffer than normal. He held out a bowl of hot stew. "I'll— It'll warm you up."

"Thank you. Smells good." She sat up, tucking her feet beneath her and reaching for the bowl and plate. "Is this homemade bread?" She sniffed it and ripped off a healthy chunk.

He nodded. "Just bought a bread machine."

Sly leaped onto the sturdy coffee table and plopped down in front of him. Her piercing gold eyes seemed to question him about why she didn't have her dinner, too.

"You'll get yours in a sec," he muttered, before leaning over and holding out a spoon for Kara. "Here."

"The stew smells so good. I can't wait to try some."

She lifted a steaming spoonful, her full lips puckered.

He couldn't turn away as she blew on the spoon, then devoured the stew. He waited, wondering what she thought of his culinary skills. When she moaned in approval, his mind spiraled in a totally different direction. His hand tightened at his side. He needed to concentrate on anything other than this infernal effect she was having on him.

He glanced back at her. Her eyes were lit up, and his chest warmed at the sight. He struggled to maintain his outward composure. Then the tip of her tongue slipped out and licked her lips. His mouth grew dry as his mind filled with the most sizzling images. A frustrated groan swelled deep inside him as he continued to stare, mesmerized by her sensuous act. Thankfully he had just enough functioning brain cells to squelch the sound before Kara realized how much power she could still wield over him.

"This is excellent," she said. "Aren't you going to eat?"

An indignant meow sounded, drawing him back to reality. He glanced down at the annoyed feline. "I'll go get yours."

He strode past the glaring cat. Right now, food was the absolute last thought on Jason's mind. The only thing he hungered for was Kara. This was going to be the longest night of his life.

If he intended to stick with his plan, his sole focus had to be on reopening the resort. Playing the friendly, considerate host was only going to get him in trouble. After all, he'd rescued her, sheltered her—heck, he'd even given her clothes to wear and a warm meal. No one could expect him to do more.

He needed to distance himself. He couldn't let his desires run unchecked, because Kara wasn't a casual-fling kind of girl. Of that he was certain. And with his past, marriage and children weren't in the cards for him. Not with Kara, not with anyone.

He had to break this spell she had over him, for her sake as much as his own. Thinking of her as just another old friend wasn't cutting it. Time for a new plan. When he returned to the living room, he'd start by reminding them both that their relationship was a professional one now... should she agree to stay on at the resort.

CHAPTER SIX

WITH THE STRAINED dinner over, Jason turned to Kara. She wasn't paying the least bit of attention to him. Instead, she was crooning over the silly cat, which was lapping up her attention as it would warmed milk.

"Kara, it's time we talked."

She scratched behind the cat's velvety ear. "With us stuck here, now probably isn't the best time to get into something serious."

"Might as well get it out of the way. There's really no time to waste."

She shot him a puzzled glance. He thought she'd have guessed he'd be extending her a job offer. After all, she'd worked her way up in the company and though he would have preferred it if things were different, she was a vital employee.

"Since you're determined to talk," she said, "get it over with."

"I want you to stay on at the resort." Her pencil-thin brows shot upward, but not giving her a chance to turn him down before he finished, he rushed on. "I want you to work for me as my assistant."

Her mouth opened, but only air came out. Why did she look as though he'd just handed her a life sentence? Couldn't she be the least bit happy, or appear interested?

"Say something," he demanded, getting to his feet to put another log on the fire.

"I...I don't know what to say. I thought you'd be replacing me, and I'd be moving on. A new town. A new job. A new life."

Did he detect a hint of regret in her voice? Was she upset because he'd messed up her plans to get out of Pleasant Valley? Was this her chance to escape, and he was standing in her way?

He knew what it was like to want to move away. Sure, when he was a little kid, things had been good at home. Back then he couldn't imagine ever leaving the Greene Summit. But his entire life had changed the day his mother died. His father's drinking had increased. The yelling and fighting quickly escalated. Nothing Jason did was right. His waning ego craved a chance to prove himself as a man. Yet he couldn't leave behind the one woman who loved him—Kara.

Swept up in his need to show the world he wasn't the screwup his father accused him of being, he'd convinced Kara to become his army wife. When she'd suggested dropping out of college and starting their adventure right away, he'd agreed. Even then he knew he wasn't being fair to her, but he'd convinced himself he'd find a way to make it up to her.

Looking back now, he realized how wrong he'd been to attempt to drag her into his messed-up life. After learning Kara had dropped out of college anyway—she'd never finished her degree—he felt awful. Another of her dreams dashed. The guilt on his shoulders doubled. Holding Kara back now wouldn't be fair to her. If moving on was important to her, he wouldn't stand in her way.

But above all, he was a businessman. The success of the resort had to be his priority. He had employees relying on him for a paycheck. And more importantly, he wasn't the only investor in this endeavor. He had people to answer to if he didn't produce a profit.

When he glanced up, the worry in her green eyes ripped at his gut. He needed to come up with a solution that would work for both of them. That would leave Kara with an out.

"Work for me at the Summit until after the New Year. Just until I get a handle on everything," he offered, even though he'd much rather have her and her wealth of knowledge on hand for a lot longer.

She eyed him. "What's in it for me?"

He couldn't resist smiling at her resilience. She would definitely land on her feet, no matter where she ended up. "How about three months' severance?"

"And?"

"And…a glowing recommendation. Do we have a deal?"

"Maybe."

"Maybe?" He jumped to his feet and turned toward his home office. "Fine, you think about it. I have work to do."

"While you're working, what do you expect me to do?"

He paused and faced her. "There's got to be something around here to amuse you. Maybe check the stash in the loft. You should find some of my grandmother's books. Feel free to bring down whatever you want. I don't have any use for that junk."

He strode away, disappointed that she hadn't jumped at the chance to stay on at the resort. Still, the worry over whether she'd accept his offer was a welcome distraction from his continual battle with his blasted attraction to her.

In hindsight, he had to concede that she was right to weigh her options. He certainly would if he were in her shoes. Now he just hoped she came to the conclusion that would benefit them both.

* * *

Kara watched until he disappeared into the shadows. He wanted her to work for him—well, temporarily. The fact he wanted her input for the reopening had her straightening her shoulders as a tiny smile tugged at her lips. The knowledge that he recognized her accomplishments was quite satisfying.

But even with this recognition, was it possible for her to set aside the past and work closely with a man who could melt her insides with one heated glance?

She'd tried so hard to put the past behind her. She couldn't let him tear down all her defenses. The surest means of doing that would be to turn down his offer. No pondering. No wondering. Just a simple "no."

Oh, who was she kidding? She couldn't just walk away—she didn't have another job lined up. How would she make the mortgage payment at the end of the month? Or buy Samantha some desperately needed shoes after her latest growth spurt?

In desperation, Kara considered turning to her parents, but they simply couldn't afford to help her out financially. Her father had been laid off last year from the job he'd held for more than two decades, and had had to take a lesser paying position with the local mall security. No, approaching them for assistance wasn't an option.

Until she found the right position, Kara had no choice but to deal with working with Jason. But for now, he didn't have to know she'd made up her mind. He could sweat it out a little while. If he thought she had alternatives, he might not take her for granted.

Eager to find a distraction, she glanced around. Her bag of knitting supplies was waiting by the front door, but Jason's invitation to explore the books in the loft was too good to pass up. She rushed over to the spiral staircase.

Their steepness forced her to slow down, having already had enough accidents for one night. At the top, she pulled on a chain hanging from a bare lightbulb, which illuminated the area. Stacks of cardboard boxes littered the floor. Surely not all of them contained books.

Like a kid on Christmas morning, she grabbed the first unmarked box and carried it to a vacant spot near the stairs. She dropped to her knees and flipped open the flaps. Inside, she found heaps of old clothes—shirts and pants that definitely had seen better days. What in the world had his grandmother been thinking, to keep this stuff?

Then a thought struck Kara. Maybe she'd stumbled across a way she could repay Jason's generosity for letting her ride out the storm here. She scampered back down the stairs and found a pen on the coffee table. Once back in the loft, she marked the box "Old Clothes. Trash."

Box after box she visually inventoried. There were old newspapers, magazines, threadbare towels and other unnecessary items. All of which she tagged for disposal.

With no more room to stack the sorted boxes, and growing tired, she pulled one last carton from the heap, hoping to at last locate a romance novel. She folded back the flaps and lifted some discolored tissue paper, to find an assortment of handblown glass balls. She grinned, feeling like a child who'd found buried treasure.

These Christmas ornaments had been lovingly wrapped and stowed away with great care. Kara vowed then and there that they would not see the inside of a Dumpster, even if it meant her taking them home.

A piece of red felt stuck between two small boxes. Intrigued, she pulled it out, to discover a stocking with white fur around the edge, with Jason's name stitched in gold thread along the instep. Her index finger traced the stitches. This had been created with love, a love she was certain Jason hadn't felt in a very long time.

He might avoid anything Christmassy, but maybe it was time he got a dose of holiday spirit sprinkled with a dash of childhood nostalgia.

Jason stared at the stack of mail on his desk with zero interest. His thoughts kept straying to the occasional sounds that came from other parts of the house. A loud thunk followed by a thump emanated from the living room. He paused in his attempt to locate where he'd placed his checkbook. Damn. What was that woman up to?

Not hearing anything else, he pulled open the left-hand desk drawer. She'd call if she needed him. He refused to accept that he was hiding from her because of the crazy things she did to his body with a mere look or a casual touch. He had responsibilities. He was a busy man with things he had to get done. He simply didn't have spare time—

Bang! He jumped to his feet. The desk chair rolled back, crashing into the credenza. With long strides, he hurried to the great room, where he blinked, unable to believe his eyes.

"Are you just going to stand there? Or are you going to help me?" Kara glowered at him as she yanked on the trunk of a pine tree that was now wedged in the doorway.

"What are you doing?"

"You told me to find something to do. I'm doing it." She gave another tug and the tree suddenly came loose, sending her stumbling back into his arms.

His heart leaped into his throat. She was soft. But her body was chilled from being outside. A longing to pull her closer and warm her up swamped his senses. This was not good. But it wasn't as if he'd done anything wrong. She couldn't hold it against him because he enjoyed the way her soft curves felt.

All too soon, she was steady on her feet. He jerked his hands away and stuffed them in his back pockets. "I meant for you to find a book to read. Not destroy my house."

She held on to the pine with one hand and turned to him. Her cheeks were rosy from the cold and begged to be warmed with a kiss.... No! Don't go there. He'd just extended her a job offer. He had to start thinking of her as an employee, no matter how much she reminded him of a sexy, tempting snow bunny.

"Since we're stuck here tonight," she said, distracting him from his errant thoughts, "I have nothing else to do...."

"We've discussed this. I don't do Christmas."

"Come on. You'll have fun stringing lights and arranging the ornaments."

His lips pressed into a firm line. "I can't think of anything I'd like less."

"Okay, Scrooge. I'll decorate the tree by myself. If you hate it, you can toss it tomorrow, after I'm gone. Okay?"

He frowned. It would keep her busy and out of his way. Ah, what could it hurt? As she said, after she left he could get rid of it. No harm, no foul.

"Just don't break anything with that bushy shrub." He started for the study.

"It's a tree—a Christmas tree," she called after him. "And where are you going?"

What could she possibly want now? He clenched his hands, his temples pounding. If she hounded him again about decorating that blasted tree, he swore he'd cut it into kindling. "I have work to do."

"Not before you help me move the table. I think the tree would look best in front of the picture window, don't you?"

He groaned. Kara smiled as though she took the utmost pleasure in his misery. With a twinkle in her eyes and a shake of her head, she turned her back on him and set to work. Once they'd moved the table, she needed a little more help. This time he had to hold the six-foot tree upright while she screwed on the base. Then the tree had to be adjusted, to make certain it was straight in the holder.

Jason clenched his jaw until it ached, holding back a string of gripes. He moved the tree this way and that way until she deemed it was in the perfect location. He knew where it would be perfect—in the burn pile. But not wanting to go another round with Kara, he choked down his sarcasm. No wonder he didn't bother with the holidays. They were a big waste of time.

"Are you sure you don't want to stay and help?" she asked, as if it was some great honor. "There's plenty to do."

He shook his head, but the enthusiastic glow on her smiling face made him wonder what he was missing. How could hanging doodads on a dumb tree make Kara glow with happiness? Although even if he didn't understand what the fuss was about, he enjoyed seeing Kara happy, he reluctantly admitted. She should definitely smile more often.

"I'll be in the study if you need me." He inwardly cringed at his choice of words. Kara could do quite well, fending for herself.

He took a few steps, then paused and turned. She'd already started digging through the cardboard boxes, lifting out smaller containers. For some reason, he was having a hard time walking away. But why? This was what he wanted: Kara occupied, so he could go off on his own. Then why did he feel he was about to miss something special?

Back in his study, Jason paused by the window and

noticed how the storm had intensified. The fallen snow was being scooped off the ground by howling gusts of wind, causing a virtual whiteout. With a disgusted sigh, he turned away.

He sank down in his desk chair and forced himself to read over the latest credit card statement. Not much later, the desk lamp flickered. At first he thought there was an electrical short, but when the light flickered again, he noticed that it affected the whole house. If they got the predicted ice on top of those winds, they'd be plunged into darkness. He raked his fingers through his hair and leaned back in the chair. Being alone in the dark with Kara, with nothing to do but snuggle in front of the fire, would be his undoing.

Her sweet voice floated through the house as she sang "Jingle Bells." Happiness rang out with each note. He could just imagine her dancing around the tree, hanging decorations here and there, a goofy look plastered on her adorable face. What he wouldn't do to watch her.

He gave his head a quick shake. He refused to let her singing draw him back to the great room. His gaze scanned the desk. Something was missing tonight, but what? His laptop. He'd left it in the other room, where Kara was pretending to be one of Santa's elves. Jason wasn't going back in there to get anything. No way. Besides, it wasn't the laptop that was bothering him.

Then it dawned on him. Sly was missing. The little black-as-night scamp usually followed him around the house in the evenings. Sometimes he wondered if the cat mistakenly thought she was a dog. He affectionately referred to her as his puppy-cat.

When he worked at the desk, she'd make herself at home on the left corner. She did it so consistently that he'd actually cleared a spot for her. Tonight the spot was empty.

Kara had not only invaded his home and his thoughts, but also had stolen his cat's affections. What was next?

Kara sorted through the open boxes scattered around the living room. Wads of paper flew. Little boxes were tossed aside. They had to be here. She started her search over again, beginning with the first box.

When her fingers at last wrapped around the crystalline icicles, she sighed. They were just what she needed to reflect the colorful lights. One by one, she attached a metal hook to the end of each ornament.

In the background, the sound of crinkling tissue paper filled the air. She glanced over to find Sly batting around a blue satin ball Kara had set aside for the garbage. The cat grabbed the small ball in her mouth and, with a jerk of her head, tossed the ornament into the air before taking off in hot pursuit.

Kara laughed at the cat's antics. If only her daughter was here to witness the shenanigans. On second thought, it was probably a good thing Samantha wasn't here or she'd start pestering Kara about wanting a kitten for Christmas—not that the subject was ever far from her daughter's lips.

Kara had started singing a round of "Deck the Halls" when the little hairs on her neck lifted. She had company. Resisting the urge to turn around, she finished hanging the icicles. She took a couple of steps back and inspected her work. Each light had been positioned with care, and then the garland had been added. And last but not least she'd used an assortment of ornaments, small at the top and large at the bottom. She'd been thrilled to find some with Jason's name on them.

"Well, what do you think?" she asked, admiring her handiwork.

Secretly, she longed for him to ooh and aah over the

trouble she'd gone to. She waited, wringing her hands to-gether as the silence stretched out. At last Jason stepped up next to her, but he remained silent. He hated the tree. She was certain of it. Her heart sank.

She turned to apologize for overstepping, and to offer to take it down, but the wonderment reflected in his blue eyes halted her words. He stood transfixed, seemingly lost in memories. She hoped he'd gone back in time—to hap-pier days, when his mother was alive.

Kara had never known his mother, but on the rare times he mentioned her it was always with devotion and rever-ence. He made her sound as if she'd walked on water. Kara used to wonder if that was what had happened to their own relationship. Had he matched her up to his mother and found her lacking?

"These ornaments," he said. "Were they in the loft?"

She nodded, but realizing his gaze hadn't moved from the tree, she added, "Yes. Do you remember them? Some have your name on them."

He stepped toward the tree and lifted an ornament of a little blond-haired boy on a rocking horse. His name was scrolled in black paint along the runner.

"I can't believe you found these."

"Surely you don't think your grandmother would have tossed them out?" He obviously hadn't glanced in those boxes to see what the woman had packed away. He was in for a surprise.

"They weren't hers. These," he said, holding the rock-ing horse ornament, "belonged to my mother."

"You didn't know they were up there?"

"After my mother died…my dad threw out everything. Pictures. Books. Anything that reminded him of her."

Kara's heart ached for Jason. No wonder as a kid he'd never wanted to spend time at that house. It'd been stripped of everything that was important to him. His mother. His past.

"Even the Christmas ornaments?" she asked, trying to keep her voice level to hide her astonishment.

"This was my mother's favorite time of year. She died the week before Christmas."

Her death had happened years before Kara knew Jason. At last she understood his Scrooge-like attitude.

"My grandmother must have known what my father was doing, and salvaged what she could." He turned to Kara. "Thank you for finding them."

She swallowed the lump of emotion clogging her throat. "I'm happy you were able to reconnect with your past." At least part of it. But there was one more thing he needed to do. "Maybe it isn't too late for you and your dad."

"Yes, it is."

Jason's frosty tone warned her not to go any further along this path, but being so ill, the man wasn't capable of tracking down his son and pleading his own case. Jason's father needed her help, and after he had helped her move up through the company, providing her with the means to support her daughter, she wanted to do this for him now. Somehow she had to convince Jason it wasn't too late to rebuild that broken bridge.

"Christmas is a time for love and forgiveness." She placed a hand on his shoulder, feeling his tension. "If not for your father, then do this for yourself. Forgive him for the past. Let it go."

He pulled away from her. "You don't know what you're asking."

"I'm asking for a Christmas miracle."

CHAPTER SEVEN

IN THE STRAINED silence, Jason helped hang a few last ornaments. All the while, he tried to understand why a bunch
of colorful ribbon, satin and molded glass should cause a
lump to form in his throat. He swallowed hard, trying to
push down the sentimental pang in his chest.

Still, his mind tumbled back in time. He clearly recalled
being an excited little kid going with both his parents to
pick out a Christmas tree. He knew his father would rather
be at home watching football, but his mother insisted they
search the mountainside for the perfect tree. Through the
snow they'd trudge until his mom gave her stamp of approval on a very special pine tree.

Of course, that had been before his dad lived only for
his next drink. Before everything went so terribly wrong.

His father, for all his faults, had loved his wife. And
he'd played along with the festive plans for the holidays,
making Jason's mother very happy. Would playing along
with Kara make her just as happy? Maybe in this one instance Jason should follow the old man's lead.

He turned to her. The expectant look on her face immediately had him uttering, "You did a great job with the
tree."

Her smile blossomed and her straight white teeth peeked
out from behind her lush lips. An urge mounted within

him to cave in to his desire to sample her sweetness—once again pull her close and see if her kisses were as good as he remembered.

"You can help me with one last thing." She knelt down next to an open box. "And what are you doing in here, little one?" She straightened, holding Sly in her arms. "Guess you don't have the same aversion to the holiday as some people we know."

Jason rolled his eyes at the cat's silly expression. And Sly's purring was the loudest he'd ever heard. It seemed Kara had totally won over his cat. What was next?

After Kara placed the cat on the quilt on the couch, she turned back to the box and pulled out an elongated container. Something about it rang a bell in his mind, but he couldn't quite pull the fuzzy memory into focus.

"I found this earlier and knew it would be the perfect final touch."

She peeled back the tissue paper and reached inside. With great care, she lifted out a Christmas angel. His Christmas angel. The breath hitched in his throat. Each year, his mother had helped him put the angel on top of the tree.

"Could you help me with this?" Kara asked, holding the delicate object out to him. "I'm too short to reach."

He accepted the angel and gazed down at her painted blue eyes, graceful wings and golden halo. The white material had yellowed over the years, but she was still beautiful. His vision blurred. Damn, dust from these boxes must be irritating his eyes. He turned his back to Kara and swiped an arm across his face.

Then, clearing his throat, he rose up on his toes and placed the angel atop the tree. He took a moment to make sure it was properly positioned, just as his mother would have insisted. Then he stepped back.

"Looks perfect," Kara said.

He nodded, not yet trusting his voice.

"I'm so glad I was able to find it. Childhood mementos can be so precious."

His gaze remained on the angel. A powerful sensation came over him, as though his mother was trying to send him a message. He knew it was impossible. Ghosts weren't real. People couldn't talk to you from the great beyond. Still, there was this feeling that she wanted to get a message to him. But what?

"It's like it's a sign," Kara said, startling him with her choice of words.

He turned to her, noticing how the Christmas lights highlighted her delicate features. Here in this setting, she didn't look like someone he needed to hold at arm's length. Maybe if he let his guard down just this once…

The lights flickered. A surprised gasp crossed Kara's lips. Then they were plunged into darkness, except for the glow of the fireplace.

"Don't worry," he said. "We've got plenty of wood to keep us warm."

"You don't think the power will come back on like it did before?"

"Not with those fierce winds. We'll be lucky to have power by tomorrow."

Even though the strings of lights on the Christmas tree were darkened, the silver garland shimmered in the firelight.

"We'll need more blankets before this night is out," he said, starting for the bedroom. "I'll grab some from the closet. They might be a bit musty, but better smelly than frigid."

Not only was he stuck with an unwanted houseguest, but they'd be a lot closer as they huddled around the fire for warmth. What in the world were you supposed to do while snowed in with your ex? Okay, well, he knew what he wouldn't mind doing....

That couldn't—it wouldn't happen. His teeth ground together. *Stick with the plan,* he reminded himself. *Remain cool and detached.*

With an armful of old blankets, he headed back to the living room. "I found these to keep us warm."

"Do you really think we'll need all of those? It's pretty warm in here already with the fire."

"For now. With the winds whipping around out there, the temperatures will plummet. The house will cool off quickly and you'll appreciate some extra blankets."

He stood rooted to the spot, watching as the light danced across her porcelain-like face. Most women looked better with a touch of makeup, but not Kara. She didn't need any paint to enhance her wide green eyes, her pert little nose or those pouty lips that always drew his attention.

Not wanting to be called out for staring, he turned around to stoke the fire. Thinking it could use another log, he grabbed one from the dwindling stack.

"I better haul in some more wood to hold us over for the night," he said, not relishing the thought.

"You can't go out there. It's too cold and windy. We can make do."

"We don't have enough logs to keep the fire going all night."

"What about your knee? It won't be good having it out in the cold."

"You've certainly got that fussing and worrying bit down pat. Your daughter is very lucky to have you." Jason couldn't be sure, but by the way Kara ducked her head, he'd bet she was blushing. "Don't be embarrassed about it."

"I'm not." She lifted her gaze to meet his. "I'll fetch

the wood. You've already done enough with getting dinner and cleaning up. It's my turn to help out."

Their gazes locked and held. At first there was a challenge in her eyes, as though she was tempting him to look away first, just as they'd done numerous times as kids. But then there was something more, something deeper. His breath lodged in his throat. He should turn away, but couldn't.

He was entranced by her eyes, seeing not only their beauty but also a hint of pain. What had put it there? Was it him? Had he hurt her that deeply all those years ago when he'd taken off for the army?

He ran his hand over his short hair. His thoughts strayed back to his time in the military, with its camaraderie and the way it kept him on the go, not leaving him time to dwell on his past mistakes. Even in basic training, there hadn't been anything they could taunt him with worse than what he'd already heard from his own drunken father.

Jason had worked his butt off, proving himself to the world. As his rank rose, his bruised ego gained strength. He was a soldier, an identity that had filled him with pride. And he'd been a damn good one…until he'd lost control. He'd let his dark side out. And the price had been devastating.

But how did he explain any of it to Kara? How did he open up to her and tell her that he was still groping around, trying to figure out how to keep his unsavory side under wraps?

Anxious for some physical labor, he headed for the door. "I'm the man. I should be the one getting the wood."

"You're the man?" Her fine brows lifted. "Where the heck did that come from?"

He sighed, realizing far too late that he'd said exactly

the wrong thing. "I just meant that you'd want to stay inside next to the fire."

Her lips pursed and her eyes narrowed. Apparently that wasn't the right thing to say, either. Why did it seem as if he suddenly couldn't open his mouth without sticking his boot in it? Military life had been so much easier. He knew what was expected of him—follow orders and don't complain. Being a civilian left him grasping for the right actions, the right words.

"Does the power outage constitute us being thrown back into the dark ages?" She planted her hands on her hips. "Me woman. You man. Let me hear you roar—"

"Hey, that isn't what I meant." He chuckled at the ridiculousness of this conversation. Definitely the wrong move, as Kara's expression grew darker. "I was just trying to be nice. After your car accident, I figured the last thing you'd want to be doing tonight is stumbling around in the snow again."

When the fury in her eyes dimmed, he breathed easier. "I'll be right back."

Sly got up from her spot on the couch. She stretched, before jumping down and running past him on the way to the door, where she stood up on her hind legs and pawed at the knob.

"Oh, no," he said. "You aren't going outside tonight. You'd blow away."

"Here, Sly. Stay with me, sweetie."

Jason's shoulders tensed at the sound of Kara calling the cat by a name she used to call him.

Just let it go. That was then, this is now.

Minutes later, a thump followed by a crash sent Kara scurrying to the door. After shooing the cat away, she reached for the handle, but before she could grasp it, the door swung open.

A gust of frigid air swirled around her, sending goose bumps racing up her arms. Jason stood there with a layer of ice on his hat as well as his coat. Purple tinged his lips while his lashes and brows were caked with snow. But it was the dark scowl on his face that had her worried.

"What's the matter?"

He shook his head, then he handed over his armload of wood, before exiting back into the stormy night with a pronounced limp. She wanted to call after him to stop and rest, but she knew he wouldn't listen. Kara ran to the side of the fireplace and dropped the split wood in a heap. They continued working together until all the wood was piled on the floor. With the door locked, barring Old Man Winter, Jason limped to the chair by the door.

"Here, let me," she said, rushing over to help him with his boots. "You obviously aggravated your knee. And it's my fault. If I hadn't insisted on you retrieving my belongings from my car, you wouldn't have…done whatever it is that you did."

He reached down, grabbing her hands in his. "It's not your fault."

"Of course it is." She yanked free of his hold and continued her fight with the iced-over knot.

"Kara, you aren't listening to me. The limp. It's permanent."

This time she stopped fiddling with his laces and stared up at him. "What are you saying?"

"Remember how I told you I have a medical discharge?" She nodded and he continued, "Well, it's because of this injury to my leg."

A sickening feeling settled in her stomach. "How bad was it?"

"Bad enough."

She needed more than that. The pile of secrets and omissions between them was unbearable. She wouldn't stand for any more. She lifted his wet pant leg up to his knee, revealing an ugly red line snaking down his calf.

The breath locked in her lungs. Her vision blurred. It tore at her heart to think of him bleeding and alone in a foreign country, miles from home. He'd had no family by his side in the hospital to talk to him, to hold his hand. No one should ever be that alone.

Jason lowered his pant leg. "It's an ugly mess farther up. So much for those sexy legs you used to go on about."

She dashed her fingers over her eyes. "Tell me what happened?"

He shook his head, once again blocking her out. "Just write it off to 'shit happens.'"

Sensing he hadn't opened up about it to anyone, Kara pressed on. After seeing the sizable wound, she knew keeping the memory all bottled up inside wouldn't allow him a chance to heal. "I'd like to know, if you'll tell me."

He rubbed his injured knee as though unearthing those memories increased his discomfort. "It wasn't anything spectacular. Just a normal day in the Middle East. Our unit was out on patrol...."

He paused and his gaze grew distant, as though he were seeing the events unfold in front of his eyes. His jaw tensed, as did the corded muscles of his neck. She wanted to reach out to him, but hesitated.

Jason cleared his throat. "My buddy Dorsy was on foot patrol with me. Earlier that day, he'd spotted a Christmas card addressed to me. The return address had a girl's name on it and he jumped to the conclusion that I had a secret girlfriend."

The thought of Jason in another woman's arms left a

sour taste in Kara's mouth. But she had no claim over him. Who he chose to spend his time with shouldn't matter to her.

"Were you and this girl serious?"

He swiped a hand over his face before rolling his shoulders. "No. I didn't even know her. Besides, I don't get involved in serious relationships. Not anymore."

"I noticed," Kara muttered under her breath. His arched brows let her know her slip hadn't gone unnoticed. "Sorry. Please go on."

"The card was from a high school student whose class had sent them to deployed soldiers. But Dorsy wouldn't drop the subject. He kept pushing, wanting to know… It doesn't matter now. The thing is I couldn't take his digs any longer. I told him to shut up, but when he wouldn't, I lost control—I shoved him."

Kara placed her hand over his cold fingers. "Yelling and giving him a push isn't so bad. I'm sure he forgave you."

Jason pulled away. "He never got the chance. He stumbled into the opening of an abandoned building, triggering a booby trap."

"Oh! I'm so sorry." The words were lacking, but they were all she had. "He was lucky he had you as a friend."

Jason shook his head. "No, he wasn't. If I hadn't lost my temper, he'd still be alive. I always end up hurting those closest to me." He paused yet again, as though to pull himself together. "Now, how about you finish untying my boot?"

Kara blinked repeatedly before making short work of unstringing his laces. "Is there anything that can lessen the pain in your knee?"

The tension in his face soothed as they moved on to a new topic of conversation. "Sometimes I use a heating pad, but without power that isn't an option."

She tried to think of a substitute. "Do you have a hot water bottle?"

He broke out into a chuckle. "Do they still make such a thing?"

She shrugged. "Hey, I'm just trying to help."

"I know. And I appreciate it."

The sincerity in his eyes sent a warmth swirling in her chest. When he smiled, her heart tripped over itself. She needed some distance. Some air. Anything to calm the rush of emotions charging through her body.

"I'll be back," he said. "I need to change into something dry."

She nodded and made her way over to the mess of wood on the floor. Work was a welcome distraction, but all too soon she had the logs neatly stacked, and had no idea what to do next. She plopped down on the couch and reached for a magazine. It was a sports issue, but thankfully, not the swimsuit edition. When she lifted it, something fluttered to the floor. A photograph.

It landed upside down. She wondered what image was on the other side. His ex-girlfriend? Did he sit here at night thinking of her? The chance that she'd been letting herself get all tangled up in old emotions while he was secretly pining for another woman left Kara spinning. The old Jason wouldn't have done that, but this new Jason she knew next to nothing about.

Anxious for an answer, she snatched up the photo. Her gaze riveted to the image of two young men with similar blue eyes and brown hair, each holding a colorful snowboard. Their appearances were so strikingly similar that they'd been mistaken numerous times for brothers.

Shaun…

At that moment, the floorboards creaked, announcing Jason's presence. He joined her on the couch. "Ah, I see you've found the picture of Shaun. Do you remember that time?"

Did she remember? She was the one who'd taken the photo.

"I remember." She swallowed hard. "We were sixteen. And life was so much easier back then."

Jason took the photo from her and held it in front of him. "Never thought we'd be sitting here nearly twelve years later, and things would be so screwed up. Back then we were the Three Musketeers. Now you and I hardly speak to one and other. And Shaun's…"

"Dead." The word pierced her chest.

"I know. It's been what? Seven years since he died in a car accident."

"How do you know about it?" She turned to him. "When you left, I thought you cut off all contact with Pleasant Valley. Or was it just me and your father you cut out of your life?"

His brows furrowed together. He reached out to her, but she scooted to the far end of the couch. "It wasn't like you're thinking."

"Then how was it?"

"When I left, I vowed I wouldn't look back. It was easy to get lost in my job, my mission. In the beginning, I'd volunteer for whatever assignment came up—regardless of the risk—but as the years passed, my curiosity about what went on back here grew."

She crossed her arms and glared at him. "So who did you contact?"

"You've heard of the internet, haven't you?"

She released a pent-up breath. "Oh."

"That's where I came across the *Pleasant Valley Journal* and stumbled over the article about Shaun's car accident. Damn shame. He was so young. He had his whole future to look forward to."

She nodded. Unable to find her voice, she thought of the boy who'd always followed Jason around, from childhood through their high school days. He'd always been there for Jason and her. Trusted, funny and dependable. Those were the traits she'd loved about Shaun.

It wasn't until Jason left town that she'd learned Shaun had been harboring feelings for her. With her being madly in love with Jason, she'd never even considered that Shaun's devotion was anything more than a deep, caring friendship. But the night Jason broke her heart at the Christmas dance, Shaun had been the one to drive her home. And again, a couple of months later, he'd been there at one of the lowest points in her life. He'd reached out to her and…

"Kara, are you okay?" Jason asked, moving next to her.

She glanced back at the photo, seeing Shaun's sweet smiling face…so much like her daughter's.

"I'm fine." Her voice was barely more than a whisper.

"It's okay. You aren't alone. I miss how things used to be, too."

The wind howled outside, while Jason's heated gaze warmed her soul. The past and the present collided. His thumb brushed over her cheek and down her neck. Kara's heart thumped madly. Could he feel the blood pulsating through her veins, making her head dizzy with need?

His gaze dropped. His pupils dilated. He was going to kiss her. Her breath caught in her lungs. This was wrong. But it'd be only once. For old times' sake. Drawn to him in the same manner a hummingbird craves sweet nectar, she licked her lips with the tip of her tongue.

His head lowered. She should turn away.

Instead, her eyes drifted closed. His mouth pressed to hers. A moan of long-held desire formed at the base of her throat. This was crazy. Utter madness. And in that moment she wanted nothing more than to be here with him, like this.

She slid her arms over his shoulders. Her fingers stroked his short tufts of hair, enjoying the texture.

His hands moved to her waist, pulling her closer. Her chest bumped against the hardness of his. Her palms slid down his shoulders, savoring the ripple of muscles. No man had a right to feel so good. She attempted to impress every delicious detail, every spine-tingling sensation to memory. She never, ever wanted to forget this moment.

His mouth plundered hers. She welcomed him with an eagerness of her own. Her protective walls fell away, leaving her open and vulnerable to this man who made her body sing with desire.

Her breath came in rapid gasps. Her hands slipped inside the collar of his shirt. His skin was smooth and hot.

"Kara," he murmured, as his lips traced up her jaw. "I want you so much."

She wanted him, too. The years peeled away. Lost in a haze of ecstasy, she couldn't form even the simplest of words. Instead, she sought out his lips and showed him how much she wanted him.

A thundering crack sent her jumping out of his arms. Dazed, she glanced around the room.

"What…what was that?" she asked, her breathing labored.

"It's okay," he said, running a hand over her hair. "Probably a tree limb snapped in the wind. As long as it doesn't come through the roof, we're in good shape."

Satisfied they were still safe in their little bubble, away from the realities waiting for them just outside the door, she turned her hungry gaze back to him. She leaned forward, eager to taste him once more. Thirsting for him like a person lost in the desert thirsts for water, she pressed her lips to his mouth.

Yet his lips did not yield to her.

They were pulled tight, resisting her advances.

Confused, she sat back.

The flames of desire in his eyes had died out.

"This can't happen." His voice was raspy and his chest heaved. "You and me. This thing. It can't happen. Not now. Not ever."

CHAPTER EIGHT

EVERY MUSCLE IN Jason's body tensed, bracing for the firestorm brewing in Kara's eyes. She yanked herself out of his hold.

"You're right." She ran a shaky hand over her mussed-up hair, failing to smooth the unruly waves. "I don't know what I was thinking. You rejected me once. Why in the world did I think it'd be any different now?"

"It's not you. I never rejected you."

"Really? That's odd. I seem to recall you making me promises of forever, and then just leaving, with no explanation." Pink stained her cheeks as her voice rose almost to a shout. "You didn't even have the decency to tell me what I'd done wrong. You never gave me a chance to fix things."

He smothered a swear word and shot to his feet, ignoring the ache in his leg. With a pronounced limp, he moved to the fireplace. He had to tell her. He had to explain the terrible secret that drove them apart—the one that would keep them apart forever.

"It wasn't you. It was me," he said, turning to meet her glare.

"Sure. Whatever you say." Her eyes said she didn't believe him.

"I already told you how I got my buddy killed. Isn't that enough to convince you that I'm bad news?"

"That was a very unfortunate accident." She settled her hands on her hips. "It has nothing to do with this... with us."

He'd have to go into the whole sordid story to make her see that his hasty departure had been in a moment of shock—of self-defense. And it had absolutely nothing to do with anything she'd said or done.

Refusing to give in to the pain in his leg, he paced to the end of the fireplace mantel, then turned, with a precision drilled into him during his time in the military. He'd never divulged his shameful secret to anyone. At least his father had done one decent thing in his life and kept it to himself. Except for the fateful night when he'd flung the gruesome secret in Jason's face.

His gut churned as the nightmare began to unfold in his mind.

Jason paused. Looked at Kara. Opened his mouth. Then closed it.

With a jerk, he turned away. The pain in his leg was no match for the agony in his chest. He continued pacing. Where did he start? And what did he do when his worst nightmare came true—when Kara looked at him with revulsion? An acidic taste rose in the back of his throat and he swallowed hard.

"Don't do this again. Don't shut me out," she insisted. "Talk to me."

"I can't—"

"Yes, you can. Tell me what awful thing drove you from your home—from me. Or is it that there isn't any secret? Did you just chicken out when things got too serious? Instead of facing me and explaining why you wanted out of the engagement, did you find it easier to bolt?"

Did she really think him such a coward? He considered not telling her, considered holding back out of spite, but that would be childish. After everything, she deserved the truth. No matter how much it cost him.

"It all happened the night I was supposed to meet you at the Christmas dance." His voice grew uneven and he paused to clear his throat.

He searched for the right words. There were none. His palms grew moist. Puzzlement lit her eyes, as though she was trying to guess what he would say next.

"I was on my way out the door when my father stopped me."

Jason inhaled an unsteady breath and blew it out. "We started arguing about his expectations for me around the resort. I'd had enough of him criticizing my job performance, nitpicking my every move. I blurted out that I planned to enlist in the army. He was livid. I'd never seen him so angry. He told me I was an ungrateful, sniveling brat and that I owed it to him to run the place."

Jason glanced up to see the color wash out of Kara's face. Her eyes were large and round, prompting him to keep going.

"I said I was tired of being a slave to a man who lived his life inside a bottle. I didn't stop there. I also told him you and I were getting married and leaving this place. He laughed in my face. His alcohol-laced breath made me want to puke."

Jason forced another breath in, then out. "He said no woman would want to marry me when she found out the truth. I told him there wasn't anything he could say or do to keep me from marrying you."

Boy, had he been wrong.

He swallowed hard, fighting back the wave of fear over Kara's impending repulsion. He wanted more than anything in the world for her to understand, but how do you understand the incomprehensible? How do you reconcile yourself to the fact that the person you thought you'd once known was a stranger?

He just had to say a little more and then it'd be out there. There'd be no more fighting this attraction, because she'd never let him get close to her again. And he wouldn't blame her.

"My father staggered up to me. He stabbed his finger in my chest and stared at me with those bloodred eyes. He told me I was an ungrateful bastard. His words were slurred, but their point came across loud and clear."

Kara's hand flew to her mouth. Her eyes shimmered with pity.

When dreadful seconds of silence fell over the room, she asked, "Why in the world would he say such hateful things to you? No parent wants to see their child leave home, but…"

"But he was drunk, and furious at me for what he saw as betrayal, for leaving him here to deal with a resort that was losing money left and right."

After seven years, the events of that night stood out crystal clear in Jason's mind. His father's words still held the power to stab at his heart, forcing him to blink repeatedly to clear the blur in his eyes.

In his mind, he could still recall his father's last blow—the one that shattered any hope he'd had of having a life with Kara. He wasn't his father's biological son. Under the strained circumstances, that should have given him some comfort—but it didn't.

The truth about his origins was so much worse. He'd run from it for so long that now there was no place left to hide.

He was the spawn of a monster.

The breath hitched in his throat. Kara would never be able to look at him the same if he told her. The thought ripped at his gut.

"Still, you were barely twenty years old," she said, drawing him from his jagged thoughts. "How could he do such a thing? I understand why you left, but why didn't you take me with you? Or at least talk to me so that we could make plans?"

With his head hung low, Jason turned away. "I couldn't."

"Why? What aren't you telling me?"

"You won't understand," he shouted.

Frustration balled up in his gut over his cowardice to spit out the real reason he'd left, the reason he could no longer be with her. He was the son of a rapist—his mother's rapist.

"I never knew you thought so little of me." Pain reflected brightly in Kara's eyes. "I thought…I thought back then that we could tell each other anything."

His vision blurred. His throat started to close. He had to stomp down these tormenting emotions. He was a soldier. He was strong. He could get through this and be honest with her.

He lifted his head. His gaze met hers. He opened his mouth, but nothing came out. The thought of her being repulsed, or worse, being afraid, silenced him.

Besides, what did it matter now? They'd both been reminded that they weren't good for each other. Nothing more needed to be said.

"I have to get some more wood," he muttered, needing to be alone for a moment to collect his thoughts.

"Right now, in the middle of our talk?" Disbelief and frustration laced her voice.

"We're going to need it tonight." He walked to the wood pegs by the door to grab his coat.

"But you just got some—"

"Not enough."

CHAPTER NINE

THE FOLLOWING MORNING, the rumble of a snowplow signaled their freedom. Jason didn't waste any time calling the towing company for Kara's car. Learning there was a considerable wait for service, he ushered her out the door. He needed to get her home. Now. He couldn't let his thoughts become any more muddled.

The ride down the mountain, though still treacherous in some places, was a far cry from the night before. Kara leaned against the door, leaving as much space between them as possible. She stared straight ahead while an ominous silence filled the SUV.

"Turn right here. My dad said they'd be at my house, checking to make sure none of the water pipes froze during the night. I can't wait to see my little girl."

Excitement laced the last sentence. Love for her daughter had filled that part of her heart he'd broken so long ago. If only things had been different—if he'd been different—he'd have a place in her heart, too.

"You can drop me off here," she said, at the foot of the long driveway.

"That's okay. Since someone took the time to plow the drive, the SUV shouldn't have any problems making it to the top of your hill."

The little white house with deep blue shutters held his

full attention. It was so small. Not that his log home was a mansion, but he'd swear her whole house could fit in his great room. How did she live in such tight quarters—with a toddler, no less? She'd constantly be stumbling over discarded toys.

"You own this?" he asked.

She nodded. "It's cozy, but it's home."

He took note of the pride glittering in her eyes over owning this gingerbread house. "It's a real nice-looking place."

"Thanks." She grabbed the door handle. "I'm sorry for imposing last night."

"I'm glad I was there to help."

The door swung open and she grabbed her things before slipping out of the vehicle.

"Wait," he called. "You never answered me about staying on the payroll until after the first of the year."

Her pink lips pursed. Little lines formed between her brows, as though the decision was a real struggle for her. He'd thought his offer had been sweet enough. Could she sense his desperation? Was she holding out for more money? Or did she simply hate the idea of working for him?

"Come on, Kara. Don't make me beg. I've sunk everything I have into the resort. If you're worried about working together, don't be. The past is behind us."

"How can you say that when I still don't know the whole story about why you called off our engagement and skipped town?"

His back teeth pressed together and his jaw ratcheted tight. Why did she have to keep harping about the past? Nothing he could say would make it any better for her; in fact, it would make things so much worse.

He gazed into her eyes and saw steely determination reflected there. She was clinging to this need to know worse than a cat holding on to a catnip mouse.

An exasperated sigh passed his lips. "If I agree to tell you, will you stay on at the resort until we have it up and running?"

"Are you still willing to provide the severance package and reference?"

He didn't want to see her go, but he didn't have any right to stop her. If she could just help him get through the re-opening, he'd be able to take it from there.

"I promise you'll get the severance package and the reference. Now do we have a deal?"

"I'm still waiting." She crossed her arms. "You owe me one more thing…?"

"You surely don't expect me to dig into my past right here in the middle of your driveway." He checked the time. "Besides, the tow truck guy will be waiting for me to guide him to your car."

She bit down on her lower lip as though weighing his words. "But you'll tell me?"

He nodded. The hum of the idling engine and the occasional gust of wintry air were the only sounds as he waited, hoping she'd see reason.

"You have a deal," she said. Before he could breathe a sigh of relief, she added, "But don't think I'll forget about your end of the deal. I expect a candid explanation from you."

"I understand."

"Then I'll see you Monday morning."

As the door thudded shut, he took comfort in the fact that there was no time limit on her request. Kara had always been persistent when it came to something she wanted, but she wouldn't be the first person he'd put off. Eventually she'd get tired of asking, wouldn't she?

A groan grew in the back of his throat. His temples started to pound. He needed a distraction. He glanced down to turn on the radio, then spotted the pink bear on the passenger seat.

With the fluffy thing in hand, he jumped out of the vehicle. "Hey, you forgot this."

Kara turned as he rushed up to her. "Oh, can't forget Bubbles. Samantha would never forgive me."

"We wouldn't want you getting in trouble."

"Mommy. Mommy," cried a child's voice. "Can we put up the Christmas tree?"

A young girl dressed in jeans and a pink winter coat ran toward them, her arms pumping. This was Kara's daughter?

Where was the baby—the toddler—he'd imagined? This little girl was so much older. She looked to be school-age. He glanced from mother to daughter. The child's pert nose, rose-petal lips and dimpled chin resembled her mother's, but there was something else. Something very familiar about her. The eyes. They were the same shade as his. So was her brown hair....

Could she be mine?

The air whooshed from Jason's lungs. The stunning suspicion bounced around in his mind at warp speed, making him light-headed.

Even though he and Kara had taken precautions when they'd made love, he wasn't foolish enough to think that accidents didn't happen.

The girl looked about the right age. His heart hammered his chest with such force his ribs felt bruised. The child had to be his.

He turned a questioning stare at Kara, but she wouldn't look at him. Did she really think she could keep his daughter a secret forever?

The little girl attempted to stop on the icy driveway and ended up sliding. Jason instinctively reached out for her. His arms wrapped around her slight shoulders and steadied her.

She eyed him tentatively with wide blue eyes. "Who are you? And why are you holding Bubbles?"

"This is Mr. Greene," Kara told her. "He helped me during the nasty storm and saved your bear from the snow."

The girl looked at him again, hesitantly at first. Then her hands rested on her little-girl hips, bunching up her padded coat. "You were smiling at Mommy. Do you like her?"

Jason choked back a laugh.

"Samantha Jameson," Kara shrieked. "Apologize."

Samantha—he liked the name. It also didn't miss his attention that the child had Kara's surname.

"Sorry, mister. Can I have my bear now?"

The *mister* part jabbed at him. She had no idea he was her father. Obviously, Kara hadn't showed Samantha any pictures of him.

He crouched down and held out the stuffed animal. "Here you go."

"Do you like Mommy?"

She was certainly a cute kid—and quite persistent. "Your mother's an old friend of mine."

Both females shot him surprised looks. Before Samantha could continue her inquisition, Kara's mother called to her from the doorway. Then, catching sight of him, Mrs. Jameson waved, a much friendlier greeting than he'd been expecting. This trip certainly had been filled with one surprise after another.

Samantha waved goodbye and ran to her waiting grandmother, oblivious to the turmoil going on inside him.

When the front door banged shut, Kara turned to him.

Her narrowed eyes shot daggers at him. "What'd you go and say that for? She didn't need to know anything about you and me having a past. Now she'll be full of all sorts of questions that I don't want to answer."

Certain Samantha was their daughter, a daughter he never knew about until now, anger bubbled up in him.

"You haven't told her about me, have you?"

Kara's brows scrunched together. "Of course not. Why would I?"

"How long were you going to keep this from me?" Betrayal pummeled him. "I'm her father. I should have been told."

"No. You're not."

"Come on, Kara. Don't lie. She's the right age and she has my blue eyes."

Kara's hands balled up at her sides. "She is *not* your daughter."

"Are you sure there's not someone else in your life?" he asked, driven to know if he'd been replaced in his daughter's life. "Someone your little girl calls Daddy?"

"No. There isn't."

Kara glared at him as though warning him to drop this line of questioning. But no amount of denials and icy stares would convince him to let go of this subject. There were simply too many coincidences to come to any other conclusion. Samantha was his little girl.

He wanted to push the topic, but backing Kara into a corner wouldn't get him any closer to his daughter. He needed a different tactic to get Kara to open up to him. And making things even more tense between them wasn't the right course of action. He needed to retreat and regroup. After things cooled down, he'd come at the situation from a different angle.

"Fine. I understand," he lied, watching the tension ease in Kara's shoulders.

What did she have to gain by continuing to deny he was the child's father?

Then it dawned on him what she was doing, protecting their daughter from him. She didn't trust him to stick around. And the fact that he was keeping the past from her was just one more strike against him.

The thought of missing out on his daughter's life overwhelmed him. For one crazy moment, he considered blurting out the awful truth. But how on earth would the revelation that he was the son of a monster—a rapist—going to help his cause? His chest tightened. The truth about his past certainly wouldn't make him a candidate for Father of the Year.

It'd be best for everyone, his newly found daughter included, if he kept his secret to himself. He'd just have to keep Kara distracted until the past was forgotten.

Besides, he wasn't the only one who'd been holding a secret. Anger simmered in his gut over being kept in the dark for so long. If the snowstorm hadn't brought them together, he might never know he was a dad.

Still, Kara thought she was doing the right thing by protecting her daughter—their daughter. The phrase stuck in his brain.

"You should get inside," he said, letting the subject drop for now. "I've got to go."

Saturday evening, after spending the afternoon scouring the internet for job opportunities, Kara sent out her résumé to five companies advertising for an office manager. Hopeful that someone would take an interest in her application, she headed to the Pleasant Valley Care Home.

After signing herself in, she paused and scanned the list of recent visitors, searching for Jason's name. No such luck.

To her utter frustration, her thoughts had dwelled on him since their winter storm odyssey. When he'd first laid eyes on Samantha, she'd noticed how he'd struggled to hide his surprise. And after he'd boldly stated he wasn't planning to have kids, she'd been shocked by his insistence that he was Samantha's father. Thankfully, he'd finally accepted the truth.

Maybe she should have explained her daughter's background, but the circumstances hadn't been right. Standing outside in the freezing cold while Samantha waited inside for her hadn't lent itself to a heart-to-heart talk. Besides, what did it matter? Kara wasn't in a relationship with him. There wasn't even a possibility of it.

After seven long years, he still couldn't face her and explain what had made him break her heart. He didn't trust her then and he sure didn't trust her now. But he did owe her the truth…and she intended to collect.

Kara's footsteps echoed through the empty corridors of the nursing home. No matter how many trips she made here, she could never shake the unease that came over her when she entered the well-kept facility. Maybe it was the idea of her own mortality—that she might one day end up here, too.

Halfway down a brightly lit hallway, in front of room 115, she stopped and gently rapped her knuckles on the open door.

"Come in," Joe's voice rumbled, followed by a coughing spell.

She stepped into the room, finding him propped up in bed with a college football game on the TV. His roommate was lying wrapped in a sheet, with his back to them and the privacy curtain partially drawn.

When Kara's gaze settled on Joe's gaunt features, her heart clenched. His thinning white hair was a stark contrast to his yellow pallor. Some people had good days dotted with occasional bad ones, but it seemed since he'd put the Summit up for sale, his days had all gone downhill.

"And how are you?" she asked, as was her habit. But she truly cared about his answer.

"Awful," he grumbled, hitting Mute on the television. "They won't let me have a cigar while I watch the game."

"You can't smoke. You're on oxygen."

His whiskered face contorted into a frown. "Didn't say I was gonna light it."

"Oh." She didn't know what else to say.

Joe had had to give up a lot of vices when his health collapsed and he'd ended up in this place. He still fussed about wanting a juicy, rare burger with fries, and the cigars, but not the alcohol. Maybe at last he realized how it'd destroyed his life.

"My boy. You've seen him?" A wet cough ensued.

Kara filled his glass with water from a plastic pitcher and handed it to him.

"I did see him. You could have warned me you sold the Summit to him." She wanted to be angry at Joe for keeping such an important fact from her, especially after all she'd done for him over the years. But it was hard to be upset with someone so ill.

He at least had the decency to drop his gaze to his bony hands. "I need you to convince him to come see me. Tell him I'm sorry."

Kara wrung her hands together. Maybe she should back out of being the go-between for these two. After what Jason had told her about what went down between him and his dad, it might be asking too much of Jason to reestablish the father-son relationship.

"I tried," she said, still not sure how to proceed. "He's very stubborn."

Joe made an attempt to reach for something on his nightstand.

"What do you want?" she asked, ready to do whatever she could to help.

"Jason's picture."

She grabbed the framed graduation photo of the boy she'd once loved with all her heart, and handed it to his father. Joe pulled off the back and yanked out a wrinkled envelope.

"Give this to him…." His words faded into a string of coughs. "Make him read it."

Her mouth gaped. How did Joe expect her to do this when Jason wouldn't discuss his father, much less have anything to do with him? But she couldn't turn her back on this man who didn't have anyone else to look out for him. She couldn't give up hope that somehow father and son would be reunited.

Joe reached for her arm and placed the envelope in her hand. His cold fingers squeezed hers. "Find a way. Jason has to know I regret what happened. Please, Kara."

CHAPTER TEN

"LET ME LICK them. Please." Samantha held out her hands for the beaters from the mixer.

"You can have one and I'll have the other." Kara couldn't resist the sweet buttery taste of cookie dough.

They were both licking at the creamy batter when a knock sounded. Sunday afternoons were notorious for impromptu visits from her parents. She continued savoring the sweet treat on her way to the door. She peered through the window, finding Jason.

Jason? What was he doing here? Maybe she'd forgotten something at his place yesterday in her haste to get home.

She yanked the beater down to her side and wiped away any evidence of her childish behavior before opening the door. When she looked into Jason's dreamy blue eyes, her heart started beating in double time. "Hi. What are you doing here?"

"Thought you might want this." He moved to the side, revealing a lush evergreen lying on the sidewalk.

"You got us a tree?"

"You said you always wanted a real tree, so here you go." He peered around her and she turned, finding her daughter lurking behind her.

"Samantha, you remember Mr. Greene, don't you?"

She nodded and moved to stand beside Kara. "Is that for us?"

"Yes, it is. Do you like it?"

Samantha's head bobbed up and down, while a huge grin showed off her pearly whites.

Kara ushered him inside. "You're letting in all the cold."

"I didn't mean to stay. I just wanted to drop this off. Unless, of course, you already put up your tree."

"We didn't," Samantha volunteered. "Mommy didn't have time. Can we have it, Mommy? We've never had a real tree. Ple-e-ease."

Kara eyed her pleading stare. "Fine. Mr. Greene, can I help you carry it into the living room?"

"I've got it," he said.

He picked it up with ease and moved forward, favoring his leg more than usual. Concern swirled in Kara's chest as she quickly ducked into the kitchen to drop off her licked-clean beater. She wanted to ask him about his leg but reminded herself that it wasn't her concern. They each had their own lives to lead, and he didn't need her nagging him about his health.

Kara held the door wide-open while he maneuvered the chubby pine through the doorway. Her living room was small and cozy. She didn't have a clue what they'd do if the tree was too big. Samantha would have a fit. But they'd cross that bridge when they got to it.

"Put it here," Samantha called, pointing to a spot in front of the window. "This is where we always put the *other* one."

Jason glanced at Kara and she nodded in approval. "Just give me a second to slide the chair out of the way."

In a matter of seconds, the tree stood prominently in front of the window, with a few inches of clearance between the tip-top and the ceiling. Kara breathed a sigh of relief. Jason had already anchored it in a red-and-green metal stand, attached to a piece of wood. All she'd have to do was add water and a tree skirt.

Samantha clapped her hands together and beamed. "Mommy, isn't it great? Now you don't have to find time to drag down that dang tree—"

"Samantha! That's enough." Kara's cheeks warmed with embarrassment. Apparently her daughter had overheard her muttering to herself in frustration at the overwhelming prospect of putting all their Christmas decorations up this weekend.

"Sorry." Samantha didn't look the least bit sorry as she grinned at the tree as if she'd never seen one before.

But when her daughter's blue eyes settled on Jason with that same ear-to-ear smile, Kara knew she was in trouble. She didn't need these two to bond. No way.

"We're making cookies," Samantha said. "Wanna decorate 'em with me?"

Jason rocked back on his heels. His hesitant gaze traveled to Kara. Working with him would be tough enough. She didn't need him befriending her daughter. She gave a slight shake of her head, praying he'd get the message.

"Thank you. That sounds great...." His gaze ran to Kara again, as though he was actually interested in spending time with a six-year-old.

Part of Kara wanted to relent and have him stay, to make her daughter happy, but she knew in the end that it'd end up hurting Samantha when he walked out of their lives. He wasn't a forever kind of guy. When the going got rough, Jason got going. *Reliable* definitely wasn't in his vocabulary.

And what was even worse was that he represented the one thing Kara couldn't give her daughter—a father. Up until this point, Samantha hadn't shown any curiosity about her dad, but the day was coming when she'd be full of questions. And Kara couldn't help but wonder if her little girl would blame her for never marrying and giving her a father figure. Still, Jason wasn't an ideal candidate.

Kara steeled herself and gave another shake of her head. Jason was a gentleman and explained that he had a previous engagement, causing her daughter's smile to morph into a frown. Kara couldn't blame her. If she wasn't careful, she, too, would get sucked in by his charms.

He walked to the door, then turned to Samantha. "I almost forgot. I have something else for you. I'll be right back."

Samantha raised her bright eyes to her mother and practically bounced with excitement. "I wonder what it is."

"I don't know." Truly she didn't, but she had to admit she was curious.

When he rushed back up the walk, he was holding a small box. It looked familiar, but Kara couldn't quite place it.

He held it out to Samantha. "This is for you, but on one condition. You have to finish baking with your mother and help with the cleanup before you open it. Can you do that?"

Her head bobbed. "Sure."

"What else do you say?" Kara prompted.

"Oh, yeah. Thank you. Come on, Mommy." Samantha pulled at her wrist. "We have cookies to make."

Jason chuckled. Kara hadn't seen him this relaxed in all the time she'd spent with him at his place. Apparently he related to little girls more easily than he did to big ones.

"Have fun baking." He waved and strolled down the walk, whistling a little ditty.

What in the world had put him in such a good mood?

"Mommy. Mommy. Look at this."

Kara closed the door and turned, to find her daughter

had ripped away the snowman wrapping paper and opened the cardboard box. "You promised to wait to open it, remember?"

Samantha shrugged, peering inside the box. "I know. But I just wanted to peek. Isn't she beautiful?"

She held up the box for Kara to get a good look at the contents. The angel. Jason's Christmas angel.

When Samantha made a motion to reach inside the box, Kara yelled, "Don't! Your hands still have cookie dough on them. Hand me the box." Samantha frowned, but did as instructed. "Now go wash up. We have cookies to finish making before we decorate the tree."

Kara carried the heirloom into the living room. What had Jason been thinking when he'd decided to give away this treasured memento from his childhood? She'd thought for sure, with the memories of his mother the angel invoked, that he'd hold on to it. This just went to prove that she really didn't know him at all.

After another quick glance at the angelic figure, she placed it atop the bookshelf for safekeeping. He might not be ready to appreciate such a fine gift from his past, but she'd hang on to it for him, until his heart was open to the joy of Christmases past and the hope of Christmases future.

Jason Greene, for all of his faults, was hard to resist when he turned on the charm. His visit today had chipped away at the hard edges around her heart. She glanced out the window, but he was long gone.

She still needed to talk to him about so many things. Not only did they have the past to straighten out, but now his father's Christmas wish was weighing on her. She prayed there was some way to broker a bit of peace between the two men. The sands of time were running out for this father-son reunion.

* * *

Jason sat behind a large, solid wood desk—the same desk where his grandfather used to hold him on his knee and tell him that one day this place would be his. That day had finally come. He'd just never imagined he'd be working alongside Kara.

His gaze lifted and met hers. He'd been doing most of the talking for the past hour, explaining his vision for the future of the resort. He'd noticed her raised brows a couple of times when he'd covered how he thought they could cut back on expenses. However, she never interrupted, just continued to take notes.

Now it was time to get to the part where she could really be helpful to him. "While I work on finding the appropriate balance between year-round and seasonal workers, I'd like you to get new quotes from all the available vendors."

"Which one did you have a problem with?"

"It isn't that I have a problem with any of them, but it's a smart business practice to periodically get quotes and make sure no one is gouging us."

She shook her head. "They wouldn't do that. We've been doing business with these companies for years now—"

"And when was the last time you received quotes from the competition?"

"Never, but—"

"Exactly what I thought. My father always did take the easy route. I'm sure that's why this place is in the red."

"I should have been on top of this. Is this really what has the business in trouble?"

He didn't want her blaming herself. "There are many things that contributed to the financial mess, but it's not one single person's fault. We're going to put into place new procedures and policies, so we don't end up in a rut again."

"Which vendors did you want me to work on?"

"All of them. From the liquor to the vegetable supplier and everything in between."

"But surely you don't want to get rid of Pappy Salvatore's."

Jason searched his memory. The name didn't ring a bell. "Who's this Pappy?"

She cast him a look of disbelief. "He's a childhood friend of your father's. He and his sons have been providing us with the freshest vegetables longer than I've been here. They're punctual and their produce is of the finest quality."

Jason paused and stared at her. Throughout this meeting, she'd accepted what he'd said about overhauling the mechanics of the place. Her occasional frown let him know she didn't always agree with his methods, but she'd kept her mouth shut. Why in the world would she pick this one particular vendor to defend? Was it possible there was more going on with the Salvatores than just business? The thought soured his stomach.

"How well do you know this Pappy? Or perhaps you're more familiar with one of his sons?"

She glowered at him. "Don't twist this into something it's not. Yes, I know Pappy. He used to come to the resort once a month to go over the order with me...and your father. He's a sweet man and his whole family is involved with the business."

Still not getting the reason for her to defend their business ties so ferociously, Jason prompted, "And..."

"And he was instrumental in convincing your father to give me the promotion to office manager. He was so impressed with how I'd reworked the various menus, giving each of our food outlets a different ethnic flair."

"Of course he was. He wanted you to swing him more business."

Her eyes narrowed and her chin lifted. "He didn't need to. Your father had already awarded him the resort's full order years ago. He did it because I impressed him with my ideas."

Jason rocked back in his desk chair. He liked this Pappy and he hadn't even met him. He also liked Kara's strong sense of loyalty. He could only wish she'd hold *him* in such high esteem one day. But how he'd manage to get there, he didn't know.

"That still doesn't put the Salvatores above review. Get the quotes. We'll talk later."

Kara's lips pursed together as her pen flew over her notepad. "Is that all?"

"There's one more thing. Could you check on the furniture we ordered for the Igloo Café?"

She nodded, got to her feet and headed for the door.

Not wanting her to go just yet, he said, "I meant to ask you if Samantha liked the tree."

Kara clasped her notepad to her chest. "She did. Depending on what time I get home, we're supposed to finish trimming it."

"There's no need for you to hang around here tonight," he said, deflated by the fact that she hadn't extended him an invitation. "I've got all the files I'll need. Go home and enjoy the evening."

Her green eyes widened. "Are you sure? The reopening isn't far away."

"Positive." He wanted this Christmas to be special for their daughter, whether Kara let him share it with them or not.

She hesitated at the doorway. Was she having second thoughts about inviting him over? Hope rose in his chest. Christmas still wasn't one of his favorite holidays, but for Samantha's sake, he could learn to like just about anything.

"Did you need something else?"

She nodded and pulled an envelope from the back of her notebook. "I need you to read this."

Disappointment hit him hard and fast. He struggled to keep his poker face in place as he held out his hand. "Is it something I need to go over tonight?"

She worried her bottom lip. "Time is of the essence."

"Pass it over and I'll give it top priority."

When he glanced at the envelope and saw the return address, he groaned. Now he knew why she was acting so strange—it was from his father.

"Kara, take this back." It'd be filled with more accusations about how he'd failed as a son. He couldn't—no, he wouldn't let that man inflict any further pain.

"You said you'd read it. You said you'd make it a priority." Her brows scrunched together as her eyes pleaded with him. "You can't pretend he doesn't exist. And you'll regret it if he dies before you have a chance to make peace with him."

Jason didn't want to hear any of this. "I'm the injured party here. My father was the one who pulled away after my mother died. He's the one who turned to a liquor bottle for comfort. He never thought of me or my needs."

"I'm so sorry, Jason. To lose your mother and then for all intents and purposes to lose your father, too, must have been devastating for you. But it's not too late to try and undo some of the damage."

"Why is this so important to you?"

"This will be your father's last Christmas." Her voice cracked with emotion. "If a person can't forgive, they can't know real love. It's a lonely life. Is that what you want for yourself?"

"You think I can't love?"

She shrugged. "Joe wasn't always a bad father. You told me."

Jason's jaw grew rigid. She was a good talker, but he just couldn't put himself out there for his father to throw all his misdeeds back in his face.

Jason held out the letter, but she turned her back and walked out of the room.

With a sigh, he leaned back in his chair as her last comment settled in. It was true. His father hadn't always been a bad man. In fact, Jason could remember a few fishing trips to the state park. They'd hardly caught a thing, but his dad hadn't seemed to mind, as the two of them talked a lot about sports. Jason had just been glad to have his father pay some attention to him.

Then his mother had gotten sick and there were no more fishing trips. It was at his mom's bedside that he first saw his father cry. That was when Jason knew his mother was never going to get better—and that was when he'd really needed a father. But his dad retreated to his study and wouldn't let anyone in. Bottles of Jack Daniel's and Jim Beam had kept him company, putting him into a numbed, drunken stupor.

"Damn." Jason threw the envelope on the desk.

Since the first night he'd run into Kara, she'd been on this blasted campaign to reunite him and his father. And no matter how much Jason wanted to please her, he couldn't do what she asked of him. Too many damaging words had been inflicted. The deep emotional wounds had festered over time, not healed. It was best to leave them alone.

He shook his head, trying to chase away the unwanted memories. His teeth ground together. This was Kara's doing—unearthing his past. She'd wanted him to remember, but it wouldn't work. This was one Christmas miracle even she couldn't pull off, with all her good intentions.

But if she truly thought he couldn't love, she was wrong. As much as he wanted to deny it, she had a permanent spot in his heart. And as for their daughter—he'd fallen for her at first sight.

Now he just had to find a way to show Kara that he wasn't the heartless creep she imagined him to be.

CHAPTER ELEVEN

MEETING AFTER MEETING about streamlining the resort's expenses kept Kara in close proximity to Jason. However, with so many other employees drifting in and out of his office, she didn't have a chance to ask about the past, and get answers to the questions that had plagued her for so many years.

If she didn't know better, she'd swear he'd planned his open-door policy as a way of keeping them from talking privately. But if he thought she'd forget about their agreement, he was most definitely wrong.

So when the phone rang on Saturday, Kara was startled to hear his voice at the other end. He was all-business, asking for her assistance in finding some pertinent paperwork. When she said that she'd have to bring Samantha with her, his tone softened and he said he had an important job for her, too.

Not wanting to give him any excuse to fire her before the holidays, Kara shut down her internet search for jobs, scooped up Samantha from in front of the television and rushed out the door.

With the late afternoon sun playing hide-and-seek behind the trees lining Greene Summit's winding roadway, she drove up to the lodge. Samantha chattered about anything and everything that caught her attention, as was normal during a car ride. Only today her conversation wasn't about school or Santa. Today her only thought was about seeing Jason.

They parked in the vacant front lot, by the main entrance. Massive timbers acted as supports for the alcove roof, while layered logs made up the walls of the lodge, giving it a natural outdoorsy feeling.

"Mommy, hurry," Samantha said, yanking on her hand. "He said I could help him do somethin' impotent."

"Important," Kara corrected, and released her daughter's hand in order to unlock the door.

Inside the newly renovated lobby, a soft pine scent lofted throughout the two-story space, thanks to the giant Christmas tree that soared up toward the skylights, lights twinkling from every branch. A musical rendition of "Have a Holly Jolly Christmas" played in the background. Since they were the only ones in the building, aside from Jason, she couldn't dismiss the fact that he'd taken time to turn on the lights and music to impress Samantha. Her daughter walked all around the tree, admiring the red and green decorations.

"Wow, look, Mommy. Think Mr. Greene did all of this for us?"

Kara smiled. "I think the decorations are for the grand reopening, but I'm sure he'd be happy if you told him how much you like them."

"I will."

As though her thoughts had summoned him, Jason strode over to them. A smile lightened the tired lines on his face. "Hi. So what are my two favorite ladies up to?"

"Waiting for you." Samantha giggled.

"I hope we didn't take too long. I had a nut roll in the oven when you called," Kara said, trying to ignore the way his smile made her heart pound.

Samantha moved to stand directly in front of Jason. "Mr. Greene, I'm ready to work. Look," she said, holding up her stuffed bear. "I brought help."

He chuckled. "Samantha, I wish all my workers were as eager as you and Bubbles."

"What are we gonna do? Is it fun?"

"Slow down," he said. "I called you and your mom here because I have a little work I need your mother to do for me."

Kara stood next to the towering evergreen, observing the way her daughter's eyes lit up as she interacted with Jason. He certainly could turn on the charm. She'd have to be careful or they'd both be vulnerable to his radiant smile and kind words—and that couldn't happen. She knew how much it had cost her when he'd changed his mind about a future with her, and moved on—alone.

Samantha's lower lip stuck out. "I thought you had somethin' impotent for me."

He chuckled, most likely at her daughter's poor grammar, or maybe the way her bottom lip sagged.

"Cheer up," he said, "I have something in mind for you. A real important job. First, would you like to see the changes we've made to the resort?"

Samantha shrugged. Kara knew she should just take care of business and leave, but she was anxious to take a look around. Since Jason took over the Summit, she'd been tucked away in the office, shuffling papers, making phone calls and attending meetings. She'd missed seeing all the renovations. What would a five-minute tour hurt?

"And afterward—" he knelt down by Samantha and whispered loud enough for Kara to overhear "—I was hoping you could help me test the machines in the game room."

"The game room!" Samantha screamed. Her blue eyes sparkled with excitement.

Kara bit back a groan. What was he up to? The last thing either of them should be doing on a Saturday afternoon was hanging out like...like a family. The thought was so foreign to her. It'd always been enough to know she and Samantha were a family unit. Kara didn't like how being around Jason filled her head with thoughts of what was lacking.

She cleared her throat, gaining the others' attention. "As kind as your offer is, we can't stay—"

"Mommy." Samantha's cherubic face scrunched into a stormy frown. "I wanna stay!"

Kara's gaze moved from Samantha to Jason's pleading look. Why was she the only person who thought this was a bad idea? Didn't he have more important things to do than play tour director?

"Please, Mommy? I already have my homework done."

That was true enough. Samantha had been an angel all week. Kara knew it had a lot to do with Santa, but she'd take what she could get, when she could get it. Her daughter had earned the right to have a little fun. Who was she to take it from her?

"Okay. But we can't stay long—"

"Yay!" Samantha cheered.

"Good." Jason smiled, setting Kara's heart aflutter. "Let's go take that tour. I think someone is anxious to begin her work."

"Uh-huh." Samantha beamed a cheery smile at them before grabbing a hand of each adult and pulling them onward.

Kara glanced past her daughter to Jason, who seemed truly relaxed and comfortable holding Samantha's hand. Letting him field the child's million and one questions about the resort, Kara took in all the recent updates.

The hallway's robin's-egg-blue walls were bare, and a faint smell of fresh paint lingered. A lifetime of memories lived and breathed inside this ski lodge. If these walls could talk, they'd spill stories of stolen kisses, tears and shared promises.

Jason pointed out the new restaurants, spa and indoor Olympic-size pool while the past continued to crowd in on Kara. She remembered how things used to be—how things might be again, if only she could make Jason understand the impossible. But her confession wouldn't fix things between them. It'd only scare him off. She doubted even this business could hold him back if he learned exactly what had happened after he'd dumped her. Not that she'd ever have a reason to tell him. He was her boss, nothing more.

The tour concluded with the game room to the left and a bowling alley to the right. A screech of joy ripped from Samantha's lungs. "There's a bowlin' alley, too."

Both of them laughed at her comical enthusiasm as she tried to decide what game she wanted to try first.

"Mister, can I really play them all?"

His smile lit up his face, making his blue eyes twinkle. "First, call me Jason."

"Jason, can we play now? Bubbles wants to bowl. Can we, huh?"

"We have a lot of games to test, so we better get started." He rolled up his shirtsleeves, then found the power switch. Lights flickered and the lanes lit up.

"Mommy, are you gonna play, too?"

"I don't think so. I can't bowl in these boots."

"Not a problem," Jason assured her. "We've got brand spanking new shoes. What size are you?"

Kara took in the expectant look on her daughter's face and then turned to meet Jason's appealing gaze. How could she turn them down? After spending way too many hours being professional, and a responsible adult, she was just as anxious as Samantha to let loose and be included in the fun.

They placed bumpers in the gutters to keep their balls in the lane. Jason and Samantha nearly doubled over in fits of laughter when in her enthusiasm Kara flung the ball too hard and too soon. It bounced over the bumper and into the next lane. Samantha, with the aid of a bumper or two, pulled off a spare, while Jason scored strike after strike.

After he soundly beat Kara, he surprised them with a takeout pepperoni pizza he'd kept warm in the employee kitchen. When he glanced her way, Kara mouthed, *"Thank you."*

He had outdone himself this afternoon. The man certainly was full of surprises. Her daughter was thrilled with the fun, and to be honest, Kara was thrilled, too.

When they finally worked their way over to the game room, Jason produced a pocketful of quarters. He handed Samantha a few. "Here you go. You can test the machines in here while your mother and I talk a little business."

"Aren't you gonna play, too?"

"In a couple of minutes." He ran a gentle, reassuring hand over Samantha's back, making Kara's heart pinch as she thought of all the father-daughter moments her little girl had missed.

Samantha, seeming satisfied to wait, moved to a claw game where the intent was to pick up one of the colorful plush animals with the shiny metallic prongs and place it in the chute. Before she could utter a complaint about being too short, Jason produced a plastic footstool. This was the thoughtful, generous guy Kara had fallen in love with all those years ago. And if she wasn't careful, the past just might repeat itself.

"Step up here," he said, holding out his hand to assist Samantha. "Better?"

"Yeah. Thanks." She surveyed the mound of colorful stuffed animals. "I want that purple monkey."

"Put your quarter in and give it a shot."

Kara swallowed back the emotional lump in her throat. No man had ever taken such an interest in her daughter. Who'd have guessed Jason's Scrooge-like heart could be thawed out by a little girl? Miracles really did happen.

With Samantha occupied, Jason approached Kara. "She's having a lot of fun, isn't she?"

Funny that he'd need her confirmation when the glowing smile and rosy cheeks on her daughter spoke volumes more than Kara could ever vocalize. "Yes, she is. Thank you for this. Since I started working overtime to prepare for the new management, there hasn't been any time to get out and have fun."

"Jason, aren't you going to play, too?" Samantha whined. "I keep droppin' the monkey."

"I'll be right there." He turned back to Kara. "Do you want to help her?"

"She wants you. But first, what file can't you find?"

He paused as though he didn't have a clue what she was referring to, then a light of recognition sparked in his eyes. "The order for the parts for the lift on the double-diamond slope. They were supposed to be here yesterday. Without a functioning lift this grand reopening is going to be a grand disaster."

He wanted an order form? On a Saturday afternoon? There was nothing he could do about the missing order before Monday morning. What had he been thinking when he'd called her? Of course, he hadn't been thinking. She'd never seen anyone work harder than Jason. He expected his employees to give their all, which she didn't mind during the week, but the weekend was for family—something he knew nothing about.

She glanced up to find he'd moved to the claw machine. His hand worked the joystick and his lips pressed into a firm line as he concentrated on grabbing the toy. Her annoyance faded. This was the most enjoyment she and her daughter had had in a long time.

"I'll be right back," Kara called out. Neither seemed interested, as the monkey hung precariously from the metal claw.

She moved swiftly to the business offices, located the purchase order and placed it front and center on Jason's cluttered desk. Her hand hovered as she debated whether to see if the letter from his father was still there. What would it hurt?

It took a little bit of searching, but eventually she located it beneath a mountain of paperwork. Still unopened. She frowned as she placed it conveniently beneath the folder Jason had requested. He would read his father's words, eventually. Hope burned strong and bright in her heart.

Jason's cheeks grew sore from smiling.

He shook his head in disbelief. Samantha hit the left bumper on the vintage pinball machine. How could this pint-size little girl clutching a purple monkey bring him such happiness?

He regretted each and every minute he'd missed of her life, but it would be different from here on out. As soon as he proved to Kara that he could keep the monster side of him at bay, and show her that he wasn't going anywhere ever again, there'd be a lot more moments like this. He'd make sure of it.

Kara strolled back into the game room. Even though she wasn't wearing anything stylish, he thought she looked positively radiant. A pastel pink sweater stretched across her chest, snuggling against her feminine curves. His mouth grew dry. And her low-slung jeans clung to her rounded hips. If he were to envision the perfect snow bunny, it'd definitely be her.

"I can see by the new stuffed animal in Samantha's arms that you two beat the claw machine."

He swallowed. "It took a few quarters but we got it."

"Samantha looks happy. Has she tried every game yet?"

"Almost." As far as he was concerned, she didn't have to leave anytime soon.

"By the way, I found the order form and left it on your desk. But the supplier won't be open until first thing Monday morning."

"Thanks. I'll straighten it out then."

"We should get going," she said. "I'm sure you've got more important things to do."

"Stay just a little longer." He reached for her hand. His thumb stroked her soft skin. "You haven't told me what you think of the remodel."

He honestly didn't care what they discussed. In that moment, he was at peace, and dare he say it, happy. Peace and happiness had eluded him for years, and he'd give almost anything for it to last just a little longer.

"You've done a marvelous job breathing new life into this place," Kara said, letting her hand rest in his. "The color scheme is cheerful and relaxing. It's a very inviting atmosphere. A great escape from the realities of life."

"Really? That's the impression you get?"

"Isn't that the impression you want to give? Don't people come to resorts to escape the pressures of their everyday lives? Aren't they here to have fun, unwind, and for some, to recapture their youth?"

Their gazes met and locked. The guarded walls around

his heart cracked. The glow of Kara's smile filtered through the crevices and warmed him. He couldn't help wondering if she was moved by the host of memories contained within the newly painted walls.

"Do you remember how we used to be?" he asked, his voice husky with reawakened desires.

A flicker of emotion reflected in her eyes. His breathing hitched as he anticipated her next words.

"I remember. How could I ever forget?"

He touched her cheek. His fingers slid down to her neck, where her rapid heartbeat pulsed beneath his fingertips. She wanted him. And he most definitely wanted her. His head lowered.

"Hey, guys," Samantha called out. "I'm outta quarters."

Jason snapped to attention. How in the world could he have let himself become so distracted that he'd forgotten their daughter was just across the room? He still had a lot to learn about being a dad.

Not willing to lose ground with Kara, he laced his fingers with hers. It felt so natural. And he noticed she didn't pull away. The pieces of his life were at last falling into place.

He glanced down at her. "Shall we go see what our daughter wants?"

The smile slipped from Kara's tempting lips and her hand withdrew from his. In that moment, he realized he'd misspoken. The shocked look on her face dug at him. How long did she intend to keep up this little charade, when they both knew the truth?

"Don't look at me like I said the unforgivable. I'm sorry I let that comment slip about her being our daughter." He paused, not exactly comfortable with apologizing. "Actually, I'm not sorry. I know you denied she's mine because

you don't trust me, but it's time we were honest with our-
selves and her."

"No!" Kara's eyes were round with worry. She glanced
over at Samantha. He followed her gaze, finding their
daughter preoccupied with another pinball machine. Kara
lowered her voice. "I wish I could tell you what you want
to hear, but...but I can't. She's not yours."

He stepped back, crossing his arms over his chest. "That
can't be. She has my eyes. She's the right age. And I haven't
seen any signs of another man in your life."

"He's not in our life." Kara's eyes shimmered. "You
don't know how many times I've wished she was yours...
but her birthday is in November. You left town in Decem-
ber. It's simply not possible."

"You'd say anything to protect her, but I swear I'll never
do anything to hurt her." He whispered the words past the
jagged lump in his throat. "Please tell me she's mine."

Kara visibly swallowed. "I can't lie to you. And I won't
lie to my daughter. You both deserve better. I swear she's
not yours."

The thought of Samantha being another man's daughter hit him square in the gut. He didn't want to believe
Kara. But the anguished look on her face drove home the
bitter truth.

This wasn't right. This wasn't supposed to happen.
They were finally reunited and...and he'd allowed himself to care about them. He'd been so close to having something he'd never thought possible—his own family. Now,
he didn't know what to do with the tangled ball of disappointment and longing churning in his gut.

"Guys, you said you'd play with me," Samantha whined,
putting an end to this painful exchange.

"One game," Kara said, glancing over at him, and he
nodded. "Then we have to go home."

* * *

The next day, Kara's phone rang. Jason's deep voice echoed over the line, making her insides quiver with excitement. For a moment she forgot she had just filled her kitchen sink with hot sudsy water to wash up the lunch dishes.

"Kara, are you there?"

The air whooshed from her lungs. "Yes. Sorry. I was distracted."

"I didn't mean to bother you. I wanted to check to see if it'd be all right if I stopped by your house this evening?"

Her pulse kicked up a notch. After yesterday, she didn't think he'd want anything more to do with her. "Um...sure."

"I found Bubbles this morning and thought Samantha would be lost without him."

He only wanted to return the bear? Disappointment pulsed through Kara. She tried to assure herself that this distance between them was best for all concerned, but it brought her absolutely no comfort.

She twisted a strand of hair around her finger. "I searched everywhere for him last night."

"You should have called me. I would have checked around here for you. As it was, I came across him in the lunch room when I was raiding the snack machine."

"You're working today, too?" she asked, astonished at his dedication and worried that he might be pushing himself too hard.

"We're making a staggering number of changes and I want to oversee everything. I need to make sure the alterations are having the effect we anticipated."

"Do you need help?" She honestly didn't have time to spare, given the scarves she had to finish knitting for Christmas presents, and more cookies to bake for the nursing home. But she felt a certain responsibility to the business that had kept a roof over her head. Plus she didn't like

the idea of Jason hiding away in the empty resort, wolf-
ing down some unhealthy lunch from a snack machine.

"I've got it under control." His voice was cold and distant.

"Samantha will be thrilled to have Bubbles back. You'll
be her hero. Not that you aren't already, after that wonderful day we had and you winning her the purple monkey."

"It's nothing I wouldn't have done for any of the other
employees and their families."

Kara's heart sank. She knew he wouldn't have gone to
those lengths for just anyone. He'd obviously been more
hurt by the news that Samantha wasn't his daughter than
he'd let on. Kara felt absolutely awful. She hadn't intended
to upset him. In fact, that was the last thing she'd ever
want to do.

"I'll drop Bubbles off at six."

Her heart thump-thumped at the thought of seeing him
again.

He'd already hung up by the time she realized he'd be
there at dinnertime. Samantha would insist he join them.
How would Jason act around her daughter now that he'd
accepted the truth? He was a man who had trouble forgiv-
ing people, but would he really punish an innocent little
girl? Kara would like to think not, but she couldn't dismiss
how he refused to make amends with his dying father.

This was her fault. She'd let him into their lives when
she knew better. From here on out, she'd have to be more
careful when it came to dealing with him. She'd need to
keep her emotions at bay—hold him at arm's length.

CHAPTER TWELVE

HE WAS LATE.

Jason lightened his foot on the SUV's accelerator. The last thing he needed was to get pulled over for speeding, and waste more time. His delay couldn't be helped. When the mechanics he was paying double time to work around the clock let him know the double-diamond lift had experienced another significant setback, he'd dropped everything to go investigate.

With the grand reopening only twelve days away, his priority had to be the resort, but tonight was different. He knew how much the bear meant to Samantha, and he couldn't stand for her to be needlessly upset. It wasn't so long ago that he'd been a child himself. He could remember what it was like to want something so badly and to have to wait. Each second seemed like a minute. Each minute dragged on for an hour. Too bad he hadn't found the little guy sooner.

The fact that Samantha wasn't his—that she belonged to another man—still had him spinning in circles. When he allowed himself to think about it, the realization socked him in the chest, making each breath painful. He should just cut his losses and move on. That was exactly what any sane man would do.

But no one had ever claimed Jason was particularly

wise. And he was already in this thing clear up to his neck. The question was, where did he want this thing with Kara to go?

And the trickier question: Could he accept Samantha without any prejudice?

The little girl was a constant reminder of how he'd messed things up with Kara. And evidence of how quickly she'd gotten over him and moved on. His fingers tightened on the steering wheel. The thought of Kara in another man's arms—a man who'd deserted her and their baby—made him furious. Jason was thankful he'd been too shocked the other night to even think of asking for the man's name. At this particular juncture, with disappointment and frustration pumping through his veins, he didn't want to do anything stupid.

His actions had already cost him a buddy's life. Jason didn't want to make things even worse for Kara and her little girl. The man might be a waste of space, but he was Samantha's father and somehow Jason had to learn to respect that fact.

He glanced at the clock. Twenty minutes after six. Being tardy would not help his already tense relationship with Kara. And until he knew what he wanted, he didn't wish to make things worse. He could only hope she hadn't noticed the time.... He shook his head. His luck wasn't that good. With her lack of faith in him, she'd probably think he'd forgotten and wasn't going to show.

When he pulled into her driveway, he noticed how she'd decorated the edges of her roof with those white icicle lights. A glowing snowman stood front and center in the yard. And in the picture window he caught sight of the Christmas tree he'd brought them, now lit up with colored lights.

The tension in his shoulders and neck uncoiled. A smile

pulled at his lips. Maybe the decorations weren't so bad. Kara certainly was filled with holiday spirit. He'd swear she was one part Santa's elf and the other part Christmas angel.

He pushed the SUV door open and eased out before leaning back inside to grab the pink bear from the seat. He glanced down at Bubbles. For a second, he envied the stuffed animal. He wondered what it'd be like to be so loved by that sweet girl.

His knee throbbed from the cold, but he refused to let it slow his pace up the walk. He'd just raised his hand to knock on the bright blue door adorned with a wreath of holly berries when Samantha pulled it open.

She stood there in a red-and-white sweatshirt with crisscrossed candy canes on the front. "Hi." Her gaze lowered to his hand. "Bubbles!"

He held out the stuffed animal to her. She immediately scooped it up into her arms and gave it a great big hug as if they'd been separated for years. He watched in wonder at the little girl's abundance of love. How could her father walk away from her?

Jason choked down a lump of emotion. "I thought you might be missing him."

Samantha held the bear at arm's length. "Shame on you, Bubbles. You shouldn't have stayed at the resort all night by yourself."

"Hi," Kara said, making her presence known. "I thought you'd changed your mind about coming over."

"I'm sorry I'm late." He opened his mouth to say more, but then closed it. He was certain telling her he'd gotten caught up in his work wouldn't warm up her demeanor.

"Step inside and close the door. It's cold out there."

Not exactly an invitation to stay, but she hadn't told

him to leave, either. Deciding to take his chances, he did as she suggested.

Strains of "Have a Holly Jolly Christmas" played in the background. The fact he even recognized the song surprised him, but it helped that the singers repeated it over and over. He didn't foresee a jolly Christmas in his future, and for the first time since he was a kid, it niggled at him.

The scent of apples, cinnamon and various other spices lingered in the air. He inhaled again, remembering how his grandmother's house had often smelled like this when she had pies in the oven.

"Were you baking?" he asked.

"No. It's warmed cider."

So much for making small talk. By the frown on Kara's face, he was wasting his time. "I should go."

"You can't," Samantha interjected. "Mommy made us wait to eat till you got here."

"Samantha, hush." Kara's face filled with color.

She'd made him dinner? The words warmed a spot in his chest that sent heat spreading through his body. It'd been a long time since someone went to any bother for him.

"It's true." Samantha continued as though her mom hadn't spoken a word. "She said you need somethin' 'sides candy to eat."

Jason chuckled. Samantha's spunk was so much like her mother's. He noticed Kara make a hasty retreat into the kitchen. Her embarrassment only made the moment that much more touching.

"Your mother is very wise. You should listen to her."

After he shed his coat and made sure the soles of his boots were dry, Samantha slid her little hand in his. His heart grew three sizes in that moment. Maybe he'd been wrong all those years—maybe someday he could be a good father. But could he be a parent to another man's child?

Could he set aside the jealousy of knowing Kara had replaced him so quickly, so easily?

Samantha gave his hand a tug, dragging him back to the present. "Come on."

The kitchen was small, but warm and inviting. He took a moment to absorb his surroundings, noticing how Kara had painted the room a sunny yellow, giving it a pleasant, uplifting feel. Sunflowers adorned the curtains, baskets lined the tops of the light oak cabinets and a small arrangement of silk sunflowers filled a blue milk pitcher in the center of the table. Kara certainly had a flair for decorating.

"Are you sure this isn't an imposition?" he asked.

"Samantha's right. We have plenty of spaghetti and meatballs. Besides, you do need to eat a real meal if you keep pushing yourself so hard to make this reopening a success." Kara drained the noodles. "Have a seat."

He pulled out a chair at the table and sat down. He looked up as Kara bent over to rummage through a drawer, and he noticed an electric candle burning in the window above the sink. It was like a beacon, calling him home.

"Mommy, Mommy, can I have more cider?" Samantha held out an empty cup, her bottom lip protruding in a look designed to arouse sympathy.

Jason would have caved faster than a house of cards in a category 5 hurricane. So when he heard Kara tell her that she'd had enough for the evening, he was impressed by such fortitude. Before he became a parent, he had much to learn.

"Go wash up," Kara said. "It's time to eat."

"Okay." Samantha scampered away.

Soon they were all seated around the table. The more he smiled and laughed at Samantha's childlike antics, the more Kara loosened up. Jason was captivated by the easy banter and the abundance of smiles. Kara had really made a happy home for her little girl. Samantha chattered on about everything she'd asked Santa for, while he made mental notes of the unfamiliar toys so he could scout around for them. For the first time in forever, he was starting to look forward to Christmas.

But the second thing he noticed that evening struck him most profoundly. They didn't treat him like an outsider. They included him in their talk, as if he was one of them. As if he was family.

After two heaping helpings, Jason pushed aside his wiped-clean plate. Utterly stuffed, he couldn't remember a meal he'd enjoyed so much, even though he'd barely tasted the food. He was too caught up by the company. Time flew by and before he knew it, he'd helped Kara wash up the dinner dishes, while Samantha watched a holiday movie. He didn't want to leave, but he also didn't want to overstay his welcome.

After he said good-night to Samantha, Kara walked him to the door.

"Thanks for staying for dinner," she said. "Samantha really enjoyed your company. Sorry about her going on and on about her Christmas list. She gets a bit wound up."

"I didn't mind at all. It was actually very helpful. Otherwise I wouldn't have a clue what to buy her for Christmas."

Kara slipped outside and closed the door. "Don't feel obligated. Santa will take good care of her."

"I'm sure he will," he said, stepping closer. His gaze zeroed in on Kara's lips, thinking they presented him with an irresistible temptation. "I would just like to do something special for both of you."

His head lowered and he pressed his lips to her warm ones, feeling the slightest tremble in her. Not wanting to push his luck, he pulled away. He caught the softest sigh from Kara. She wasn't as immune to him as she'd like to think.

He cleared his throat. "Thank you for tonight."

She pressed a hand to her lips and glanced up at him. Their gazes held for a moment before her hand lowered. "We're baking cookies on Wednesday after work and making up trays of them to take to the care home. If you aren't busy you could help."

Things weren't running as smoothly at the resort as he'd like, but he'd work day and night if it meant spending another evening in this gingerbread house with these two lovely ladies.

"Count me in."

At last, Wednesday arrived. Jason glanced down at the bag of goodies on his office desk. He'd run out at lunchtime to buy them for tonight's cookie-baking endeavor. The jaunt to the mall had taken him most of the afternoon, but it'd been worth it.

"Here's the report on the latest quotes we have from alternative vendors." Kara set the spreadsheet on his desk and gazed at him. "So what put the cat-who-ate-the-canary look on your face?"

He cleared his throat, trying not to smile, but found it to be a challenge. "I don't know what you mean."

Her brows arched. "Okay, well, these are the latest figures we received. There's only one vendor, Biggest Wholesales, who's beating out Pappy Salvatore's prices."

"Good. I'll have a look." Jason noticed the frown on her face. "You know it's best for the Summit."

"It's not that. It's Biggest Wholesales. I've heard some things about them."

If he was thinking of switching their food services to another supplier, he was smart enough to know he had to be concerned about more than just the bottom line. Sometimes the cheapest wasn't always the best.

"What have you heard about them?"

"That's just it, I can't remember. But it's chewing at the back of my mind. I'm sure it'll come to me eventually."

"Let me know when you recall. And maybe you could do some checking around about them."

She stepped toward the door and pushed it closed before turning back to face him. "Are you still coming over this evening?"

"Wouldn't miss it for the world. I have a date with a cutie to keep—make that two of them." When Kara smiled, he couldn't hold back a grin of his own. "I'll stop by your desk when I finish up here."

"My desk—for what?"

"I thought we could leave together, as long as you don't mind stopping for dinner." He really liked the thought of ending the workday and going home with Kara. It seemed natural, something he could get used to.

"But we can't," she said, a look of horror on her face. "What would people think?"

He shrugged. "Does it matter what they think?"

The fact he'd been able to utter those words and truly mean them stunned him. For so many years he'd stayed away from here, worried about what people would think of him. But now things were changing—he was changing. With Kara and Samantha in his life, he realized he was more than just the genetics that created him—he was a man with wants and needs that surpassed any gossip.

"I care what my coworkers think." Kara tilted up her chin. "They'll start saying we're a couple. I don't want that."

Jason's chest tightened. "You don't want what? Us to be a couple? Or for people to talk about us?"

"I...I don't know. Both I guess." But her gaze didn't meet his. "We still have unresolved issues."

He hadn't forgotten. He just needed a little more time before he tested the ultimate strength of their relationship. And his invitation for Christmas-cookie detail was going to help his cause.

"What are you smiling about?"

"Uh, nothing. Don't worry. I'll be discreet when I leave in about..." he glanced down at the work on his desk "...about a half hour. Do you have a preference for dinner?"

She shook her head. "But that isn't necessary. I can throw something together."

"You'll have your hands full, baking. Dinner is the least I can do."

Just as promised, a half hour later, not caring that he hadn't responded to the last five emails in his in-box, Jason shut down his computer and promised himself that he'd be in early the next morning to deal with them.

On the way to Kara's house, he made a detour to pick up an assortment of sandwiches and side orders from a little mom-and-pop shop. The restaurant been around since he was a kid, and he loved the homemade food.

Armed with food and gifts, he pulled into Kara's driveway, his heart tap-dancing in his chest. Jason didn't know much about making Christmas cookies, so he felt a bit out of his element, but he swallowed hard and climbed out of the SUV. He'd just made it to the sidewalk when the front door swung open and Samantha appeared. With the door left wide-open and a toothy grin on her sweet face, she ran up to him.

"You came! I knew you would," she said excitedly.

"You doubted my word?"

She shook her head, swishing her brown ponytail back

and forth. "Mommy said you might not come. I told her you would."

So Kara still didn't trust him, not even to keep his promise for an evening of Christmas-cookie baking. Seemed tonight he'd have to make certain she knew he intended to stick around. The thought of making it permanent floated into his mind, but he still had his doubts about taking on the role of father.

What would Samantha call him? Jason? Daddy? Did he even want her calling him Daddy? After all, he didn't know much about being a good parent. The throbbing of an ensuing headache had him rubbing his forehead. Now wasn't the time to contemplate "forever."

"Jason, hurry." Samantha grabbed his free hand and started to pull him toward the kitchen. "We have to make the cookies."

"Not so fast," Kara said from the doorway. "We're going to eat first."

"Ah, do we gotta? Jason, are you hungry?"

He might not know much about kids, but only a fool would insinuate himself between mother and daughter— and he wasn't that foolish. "We better listen to your mother. She knows what's best."

He glanced up to catch a look of approval on Kara's face. He schooled his features to hold back a grin, but his chest puffed up just a little. Score one point for him tonight. If only he could keep it up the rest of the evening, he'd definitely be in Kara's good graces, and those kisses would become reality.

Kara ushered them out of the cold and in no time they were working their way through a chicken Parmesan sub, an Italian sub and a meatball sub. Seemed as though he'd found something each of them would eat. He sighed in relief. They were off to a very good start.

With everyone's stomach filled, he pulled out his bag of goodies. He handed a ruffled, white apron to Kara that read: Don't Mess with This Cook, I Carry a Rolling Pin… and I Know How to Use It.

She laughed. "And let that be a warning to both of you."

"Do I get one, too?" Samantha stretched her neck, trying to peer in the bag.

"Hmm…let me see." He took his time, as though unable to find anything.

"You forgot me?" she asked, sounding dejected.

Then he pulled out a smaller pink apron that read: Professional Taste Tester. It also had the picture of a chocolate chip cookie with a big bite taken out of it.

"I love it!" Samantha moved over and threw her arms around his neck. "Thank you."

Jason's heart thumped hard against his chest as he tenderly hugged her back. In that moment, the thought of forever got just a little less scary.

"You're quite welcome."

And last but not least, he dumped the bag on the table and a large assortment of cookie cutters spilled out. "I bought every single kind they had in the store. I can take them back if you don't want them."

The girls oohed and aahed over the various shapes, from Christmas trees to reindeer. He smiled broadly. He thoroughly enjoyed making them happy. Once the new cookie cutters were scrubbed up, they set to work making cookies for trays to deliver to the care home where Jason's father was staying. Jason tried to block out the image of his once strong dad, now sick and needy. Uneasiness laced with guilt churned in his gut. No. He refused to let that man steal this wonderful evening from him—he'd already missed so much.…

Kara was in charge of rolling out the already made and

chilled cookie dough, as well as working the oven. That left him and Samantha to do the decorating. Bowls of various colors of icing lined the table. In addition, there were red, green and white sprinkles of varying shapes and sizes. Kara certainly seemed to think of everything.

"What's that?" he asked, gesturing to the cookie Samantha was about to decorate. "A pony?"

She giggled. "Mommy, he doesn't know what a reindeer looks like."

"He doesn't. Well, I guess you'll just have to teach him these things."

"See? These are the antlers." Samantha grew serious and pointed to the cookie. "And if I put this red ball on its nose, then it's Rudolph."

Every time the child smiled it was like warm sunbeams hitting Jason's chest. He couldn't resist a bit more teasing. "I don't know. Still looks like a pony with a bad cold."

The sweet chimes of Samantha's laughter pealed through the kitchen. Even Kara was smiling and shaking her head. He had no idea until that moment how rewarding he found the sound of laughter from these two special ladies. So why was he hesitant to lay the whole truth on the line with Kara? Why couldn't he take the next step necessary to ensure he didn't lose her, now that he'd broken through her stony barrier?

"What's that?" Samantha scrunched up her button nose and pointed at the cookie he was currently smearing icing on.

"It's Santa Claus."

She shook her head. "Santa doesn't wear green."

He glanced down and realized his thoughts had meandered, and he'd accidentally grabbed the bowl of green icing. "Well, my Santa wants to be different."

"But Santa can't be green."

"He can't, huh?" Without thinking about the trouble he'd be in with Kara, he dipped his finger in the green icing and dabbed his fingertip on Samantha's nose.

Her mouth gaped open. Her eyes rounded with surprise. It took only a second for the shock to subside. She dunked her finger in the same bowl and reached out, giving him a matching green nose. They both started to laugh.

"What are you two up to?" Kara turned and he braced himself for a stern lecture. "You're supposed to decorate the cookies, not each other." With a smile tugging at her very kissable lips, she turned to check the oven. It appeared he and Samantha weren't the only ones enjoying this evening.

By eleven o'clock, Samantha was asleep in bed and they had just finished wrapping the cookie trays. Kara walked him to the door. "Thank you for all the help. We couldn't have gotten so much done tonight without you."

"I'm glad I could help. Samantha is a great kid. And her mother isn't so bad, either." Thoughts of kissing her bombarded his mind.

"She isn't, huh?" Kara smiled up at him and that was all the encouragement he needed.

He pulled her to him. With their lips a hair apart, he paused. When she didn't move, he brushed his mouth over hers. She tasted sugary and delectable. It surprised him when she didn't resist his advances. In fact, she sidled up against him, chest to chest, lip to lip. He moaned. This was the sweetest torture he'd ever experienced. He'd been wrong—kissing Kara wasn't enough to appease his mounting desires. In fact, it just made him want her even more.

"Let's go back inside," he murmured.

Kara's hands pressed against his chest. She tilted up her chin. "Are you ready to talk about the past?"

Part of him was willing to say anything just so this

moment wouldn't end. It'd been so many years since he'd made love to her…but tonight wasn't the right time.

If he was to stay here and make love to her, it would be tantamount to declaring that he was ready to spend forever with her, and he just wasn't there yet. Kara and Samantha were a package deal, and until he was ready for all that it entailed, he'd be left with nothing but sweet kisses at the door.

"I should go."

"You know you could stop by tomorrow and we could deliver the cookie trays to the care home—"

"I can't." He just couldn't go, knowing his father was there. Not even for Kara. "I still have a ton of stuff to do before the resort's grand reopening."

Her smile faltered. "I understand."

"But I'd like a rain check. How about Friday I take you and Samantha out to see a holiday movie?"

The smile came back and lit up her eyes. "You have yourself a date."

CHAPTER THIRTEEN

FRIDAY EVENING, KARA loosened her seat belt, allowing her to twist around in the passenger seat of Jason's SUV to check on Samantha. The little girl's head had lolled to the side and her eyes were closed. The hint of a smile still pulled at her lips, while bits of buttered popcorn dotted her chin.

It had been quite an evening, with dinner out followed by an animated Christmas movie. In fact, the whole week had left Kara breathless, from her phone interview for a promising junior management position in Ohio, to letting her guard down with Jason and remembering what a good friend he could be.

She tried telling herself that with things improving with him, she wouldn't lose her job. But she couldn't hang her and her daughter's future on wishful thinking. Not only hadn't he mentioned the possibility of her staying on at the Summit, but they still had so much left unsaid between them.

She'd put off talking to him about what had happened all those years ago, thinking that once he understood he wasn't Samantha's father, he wouldn't be back. But he'd surprised her. He'd been so thoughtful, so attentive. Now that this thing between them no longer seemed so casual, she had to tell him the whole story. Her insides shivered with anxiety.

Although it really worried her that Jason was unwilling to forgive his father. Would he be as unforgiving with her when she explained the circumstances of Samantha's birth? The soda and popcorn she'd had at the theater suddenly didn't sit so well in her stomach.

At her house, Jason carried Samantha inside.

"I've got it from here," Kara said, taking hold of her daughter.

His searching gaze went from her to Samantha and back. "I should get going—"

"No." She wanted to get this talk over with, now that she'd finally worked up the nerve. "Stay, please—unless you have someplace to be."

He shook his head.

"Good. You can wait in the living room while I tuck this little one into bed. I'll be right back."

"But Mommy, I'm awake."

Kara let her stand on her own, but made sure to grab her hand, not wanting her to scamper away. "You're still going to bed. It's way past your bedtime."

"Aw, Mom."

"No 'aw, Mom' with me. Scoot."

Samantha yawned and headed to her room. The lack of protest told Kara her daughter was beyond exhausted. She'd be asleep in no time. Once they got her teeth brushed, her clothes changed and the covers turned down, Samantha begged for a bedtime story. Kara firmly believed reading to children should be a priority, but she had really hoped Samantha would be too tired to notice tonight.

"Read me 'The Night Before Christmas.'" Samantha sent her a pleading look.

"But sweetie, Jason is waiting for me." Kara pulled the pink comforter up and tucked it under her daughter's arms.

"He can read to me."

What? Jason reading to her daughter? No, not tonight. Before they got any closer, Kara had to talk to him—had to set things straight.

"Jason! Jason!"

"Samantha Jean, quit screaming," Kara said in a stern but hushed voice.

In the next moment, she heard hurried footsteps in the hallway.

"Is something wrong?" He peered into the room.

"Will you read me a story?" Samantha held up the Christmas storybook while clutching Bubbles with her other arm. "This is my favorite."

He looked at Kara. At this point, she supposed making a fuss would only cause more problems. She nodded her consent. She took a seat at the foot of the twin bed while he approached Samantha and accepted the book.

"Sit by Mommy," her daughter insisted.

His glance met Kara's and she nodded again. She scooted over and he eased down beside her. His thigh brushed hers. The heat of his body permeated her jeans, warming her through and through.

He opened the book and cleared his throat. Samantha settled back on her pillow as his lyrical voice read each line with intensity. Kara closed her eyes and listened. His voice wrapped around her with its warm tones, like a plush blanket being draped around her shoulders.

The coziness of the situation swept over her. She longed for it to continue forever. *Don't get too comfortable.* She forced her eyes open. Tonight might be the last time they saw Jason. If he couldn't handle the truth behind Samantha's birth, he'd bolt—like last time.

When Jason flipped to the last page, Samantha let out a great big yawn. Kara peered around him and witnessed her daughter's struggle to keep her eyes open.

"The end." He closed the book. "Time to go to sleep."

Kara saw this as the perfect opportunity to put a little distance between them. She slid off the bed and took the book from him.

"Aw, one more, please," Samantha whined, but without her usual enthusiasm.

Another yawn escaped her lips and Jason chuckled. "Maybe another time."

Kara replaced the book in her daughter's abundant collection and turned to find Jason standing in the doorway, waiting for her.

She straightened the covers once more and hoped he didn't notice the slight tremble in her hands. It was time for the "talk." Time to clear the air. Suddenly it no longer seemed like such a good idea. Like her daughter, she enjoyed Jason's company—but she'd already delayed telling him for way too long.

After a kiss and an "I love you," she flicked off the light. She turned and caught the warmth glowing in Jason's eyes. Reading a story to Samantha had gotten to him, too. Kara's fate was sealed, but she had to make sure he understood about this family he was insinuating himself into. This time around she didn't want secrets or omissions to come between them.

She followed him to the living room. When he stopped to turn on the tree lights, she nearly ran into him.

He turned to her and stroked his thumb down her cheek. "Thank you for sharing the evening with me. You have no idea how much it meant to me."

Her mouth went dry and she swallowed hard. "Samantha...she likes you, too. A lot."

His finger traced Kara's jaw. Her heart pounded in a most irregular rhythm. "I like her, too." He stepped closer. "And I really, really like her mother."

Drawn into this enchanting spell, she heard herself utter, "And her mother really, really likes you."

In the soft glow of the Christmas tree, her gaze locked with his. Common sense warred with her body's desires. With her exhausted daughter tucked in bed, her plans for talking began to give way to the crazy sensations Jason evoked in her. Why ruin such an enchanting evening?

His hand slid to the back of her neck as his head lowered. His lips gently brushed hers, but the restrained eagerness was undeniable. She wanted him more than she'd thought possible. And his hungry kisses were so much better than her dreams.

Snuggling closer to him, she trailed her hands behind his neck. Her soft curves pressed to his rock-hard body and a moan escaped her lips.

Suddenly, Jason grabbed hold of her shoulders and held her at arm's length. In a passionate haze, she sent him a baffled look. He wanted her as much as she wanted him, so what was the problem?

His breathing was heavy. "Remember how I owe you an explanation about my leaving?" When she nodded, he continued, "I think you better hear it now...before we go any further."

The seriousness in his voice and the worry in his eyes sent an arrow of alarm piercing her chest. She wanted to talk to him, too, but something told her that if he didn't get this off his chest now, he might never do it.

Jason drew an unsteady breath. He'd been thinking about this talk all week. And he didn't see where he had much choice. Kara deserved to know what kind of man she was getting involved with before they took this relationship to the next level—something he'd come to desire with all of his being.

But first, he had to give Kara the facts—every last horrid one. He knew he was kidding himself. She would despise him once she knew everything, and toss him to the curb. Still, since he'd been spending time with her, he was starting to believe in miracles. He had to at least take the chance, even if it was a long shot.

Kara perched on the edge of the couch and looked at him expectantly. "It's okay. Whatever you have to say, we'll work through it."

He really wished he could believe her. With his shoulders pulled back, he said, "Remember the fight between me and my father?" She nodded and he went on. "There was more to that argument than I told you…. My father was drunk, and livid that I was leaving him to deal with the resort on his own."

She didn't interrupt, even though part of Jason wished that she would. Facing combat and his own mortality had been easier than what he was about to do.

He paced the floor, searching for the exact words. When he found them, he stopped in front of her. "He told me no son of his would abandon him like I was about to do. He yelled that I was not his son…that I never had been and never would be." Jason's voice caught and he swallowed hard. "He said I was the spawn of a monster."

Kara pressed a hand to her chest as her eyes shimmered. "How horrible."

Jason's head hung low. "There's more. He told me no woman would ever accept me as a husband, much less want me for the father of her children."

He forced himself to stand ramrod straight, his shoulders rigid. He drew on the discipline hammered into him over the course of his military career. He would complete his mission.

"My mother was raped...just after my father met her." Jason ignored Kara's horrified gasp and kept going, or he'd never get it all out. "I was the consequence of her rape. My dad is not my biological father. Some unidentified monster brutally attacked my mother and..." His voice cracked and died in his throat.

In an instant Kara was standing in front of him. Her arms wrapped around his shaking body, pulling him close. The self-loathing and pain surfaced. In her embrace, he let himself feel everything he'd kept bottled up for years.

Kara held on to him, whispering words of comfort. He desperately wanted to believe it'd be all right, but it wouldn't be. It couldn't be. There was no way to rip that bastard's DNA from his body.

But now it was all out there. In the open. Kara knew he was damaged goods, inside and out. Jason pulled back and turned away to swipe his flannel shirtsleeve over his cheeks. Now it was time to face the moment he'd been dreading for years, seeing the repulsion in her beautiful eyes.

Suck it up, soldier. Facing her can't be avoided. Get it over with and move on.

He lifted his head, pulled his shoulders back and turned. With him towering above her five-foot frame, his gaze shot over her head.

Look down, soldier. One glance and it'll be done. The damage will be evident.

He forced his eyes down over her rumpled hair—hair he'd only moments ago been running his fingers through. The air became caught in his lungs. His gaze skimmed her forehead, passed her gathered brows and settled on her eyes, which held no hint of repulsion or disgust.

How could that be?

Kara stood there, returning his stare, as though he was the same man she'd always thought him to be.

"Say something," he ordered. He wanted this over. It'd already dragged on for too many years.

"I'm sorry…"

"Sorry? For what?" This wasn't making any sense.

"For your father being so horrible to you. Obviously you were never meant to know any of that. I'm sorry that in a drunken rage he'd say such hateful words."

Jason's gaze bored deeply into hers. He had to be missing something. "Do you understand what I said? My biological father is a rapist. A monster. And I have his blood pumping through my veins."

Empathy glistened in her eyes. "You're nothing like that man. You're the son of a very wonderful and loving woman."

He recalled his mother and her eternal smile. She had always been an upbeat person. His dad used to refer to her as a Mary Poppins wannabe. Always looking for the good in people. And she'd most definitely loved him.

"Can you honestly say you don't see me differently?"

"You had no control over your conception. And your mother loved you. She never held the past against you. So why should I? You're nothing like your biological father."

Jason took a hesitant step toward Kara, watching for any sign of fear in her. She didn't budge. Her steady gaze continued to hold his.

"You really believe I'm a good guy, inside and out?" His breathing stopped as he waited for her ultimate decision.

She stepped up to him. Her gaze never wavered as her hand reached out and caressed his cheek. "Absolutely."

With a smile, he swept her up into his arms and held her tight. With her feet suspended, he swung her round and round. In that instance, he knew what he wanted—what he'd always wanted.

"Jason, there's more we need to talk about."

CHAPTER FOURTEEN

KARA NEEDED TO get this over with as soon as possible. But before she could utter another word, Jason's lips were pressed to hers. She should pull away so they could finish talking, but after what he'd just told her, she didn't have the heart. He needed to know without a doubt that he was still worthy of love.

As the kiss intensified, desire flooded her body and short-circuited her best intentions. For so long now she'd been holding herself back from him, but no longer. She met his kiss with a burning heat of her own. Her arms wrapped around his trim waist, pulling him to her. His body was hard and solid against hers. She could barely believe this was happening, that he was holding her close again.

She'd dreamed of this moment for years, never believing it'd happen. Perhaps her fairy godmother was lurking in the shadows of the Christmas tree, waving her magic wand.

Jason sank down onto the couch, pulling Kara with him. His lips still teased and taunted hers. He tasted buttery, like the big tub of popcorn they'd shared at the theater. She traced his lips with her tongue, savoring the added saltiness.

His kisses trailed up her jaw to her earlobe, where he probed and tickled her, sending waves of shivers down her spine. His fingers played with the hem of her sweater, sneaking underneath to her bare waist. More goose bumps swept over her skin.

He stopped kissing his way down her neck long enough to say in a breathy voice, "We've wasted too many years apart. Marry me?"

"What?"

She yanked herself out of his embrace. He couldn't be serious, could he? Her breathing still rushed, Kara moved to the far end of the couch, trying to gather her composure. She straightened her clothes before running a hand over her hair.

"That's not exactly the reaction I was expecting."

"You're serious?" When he nodded, she continued, "You're not just getting caught up in the moment?"

A broad smile lit up his eyes. "It shouldn't be that big of a shock. After all, this isn't exactly the first time I asked you."

"But there's Samantha to consider."

"I know. But you said the biological father isn't part of her life. We'll just petition him to relinquish his rights." When Kara didn't say anything, Jason squeezed her hand. "Will the man give us problems?"

The backs of her eyes stung and Jason's image blurred. "Not like you're thinking. But there's something important you need to know."

Jason's gut churned as it used to do when he was out on patrol in hostile territory. Right now his internal radar system was telling him to duck for cover.

Until this moment, he didn't understand how much Samantha had come to mean to him in such a short period of time. Only a couple of months ago, if someone had told him he was a father, Jason would have been in total denial. Now, he'd no more be able to deny his connection to

Samantha than he could deny his love for her mother. He was more than ready to step up and accept a role in Samantha's life—in both of their lives.

"We'll deal with it together," he said, with all the confidence in the world. "What's the guy's name?"

He'd had long enough to come to terms with Samantha being another man's child. He didn't like it, but at least now he could think about it without losing his temper.

"You don't understand…."

"I know this is hard, but just tell me his name."

Kara's face paled to a sickly white, and her bottom lip trembled. "Before I do, there's something you have to understand."

The raw emotion in her eyes ripped at his gut. Jason stood on the cusp of losing the future he'd come to dream of—the future he desperately wanted. His arms dropped to his sides and his hands clenched into tight balls. *No, this can't be happening.*

"Don't do this." The hoarse words tore from his throat.

A single tear dropped onto her cheek. She swiped it away.

"I'm sorry, but you need to hear the truth—the whole truth."

He was a man who'd been on the front line of combat, who'd faced the enemy and never considered backing down. But at this moment, he wanted to make a hasty retreat. His eyes searched out the door, yet his feet wouldn't cooperate. Running from the truth wouldn't change it.

"Whatever you have to say, I can deal with it," he said. He had to.

He loved them.

The revelation stole the air from his lungs. He wanted Kara and Samantha more than he'd ever wanted anything in his life, including restoring his family's resort.

He couldn't let this thing between them end before it had barely begun.

Surely whatever she had to say couldn't be nearly as bad as what he'd told her. Kara was just overreacting. If she could forgive and accept him, then he could do the same for her now. After all, wasn't that the foundation of a good relationship—being able to forgive each other?

"When you left—" Kara's voice cracked. She started again. "After you'd ended our engagement with no explanation, I was devastated."

She pressed her lips together and swallowed. "For a couple of months I hid in my room. I cried my eyes out, trying to figure out what I'd done wrong to make you leave. I hoped and prayed you'd change your mind and come back for me." She paused, sucking in an unsteady breath. "I even asked your father for your phone number or address, any way I could get in contact with you."

"I didn't let him know where I was stationed. I even changed my last name, to make it impossible for him."

"Your father sounded so broken up when he told me he hadn't heard from you. I was totally lost and I hurt so badly. My friends rallied around me. They said I needed to forget you and get on with my life. They insisted I go out with them to a party. But they didn't understand. How could they understand what you and I shared?"

Her words were like a sledgehammer, beating at his chest. Jason opened his mouth, searching for an apology. Unable to find words to express the depth of his regret, he closed his mouth. She wouldn't even look at him now. Her hands were clenched in her lap. He wanted to reach out to her, but his nerve faltered.

Kara had never been a partier. She'd much rather be doing outdoor sports than watching her friends get drunk.

Something must have happened at that party. His chest struggled for each breath as he waited.

The silence flowed on. Her pink lips trembled. He'd always been drawn by them. Surprised he'd noticed them now of all times, he continued to stare. The temptation to smother them in a reassuring kiss and erase the rest of this doomed story overrode his apprehension. He stepped forward. Maybe just one kiss could change this perilous course they were on, but logic told him it'd only delay the inevitable. This journey had been preordained years ago.

He pulled his foot back and took a firm stance. "Kara, whatever it is, just say it."

"At the party," she said, giving him a hesitant glance, "I found a dark corner and stayed there. I regretted going, but since I hadn't driven, I had to wait for my ride. Anyway, someone decided I needed to loosen up, so they spiked my drink. When I realized what they'd done, I hesitated. I wasn't thinking clearly, but they convinced me that the drink would take the edge off the pain."

She paused, her eyes not meeting his. One by one, each muscle in his body grew rigid, while a sickening feeling brewed in his gut.

"I was young and stupid. I don't have any other excuse for what happened next. One drink led to another and another. You know I didn't drink, so it didn't take long before I was feeling good—too good." She rubbed her hands together. "Shaun showed up. Someone had called him when they found me wasted. He took care of me…."

Jason's uneasiness ramped up to an excruciating pain, as though he'd been riddled with bullets, left on the side of the road to die a slow, agonizing death. He wanted to be there for Kara, just as she'd been there for him, but this… this was different.

"I was wrong," he said, his voice hoarse. "I don't want to hear this."

He took a step toward the door.

"You have to listen." The eerie, high-pitched tone of her voice put a stop to his retreat. "You can't run away. Not this time."

His teeth ground together. His jaw flexed. The door was in sight, but the determination in Kara's voice told him that she'd follow him this time. He summoned up the courage he'd clung to on the battlefield, and turned.

Kara stood now. Her gaze held his with a fierce determination. "You weren't there to help me—but like always, Shaun filled in. He was your lifelong best friend. We had been the Three Musketeers. I trusted him almost as much as I trusted you."

She dashed away another tear. "He attempted to sober me up. He took me to his car, intent on getting me home."

Jason felt trapped on a runaway train. His life whizzed past him and there was no way to get off. He could only hold on, bracing for the devastating collision with the truth.

"On the way, I started to cry. Shaun pulled off on one of the desolate country roads. It was late and there wasn't any traffic. He tried to comfort me—"

"Stop." Jason's voice thundered in the room. He couldn't bear to hear any more.

The stabbing pain in his chest had him glancing down, searching for blood. He took a moment to gather his shattered illusions.

"Shaun is Samantha's father?" he asked, stumbling to latch on to this fact.

Kara nodded. Silent tears streamed down her cheeks. "Yes, he is."

The brown hair and blue eyes made sense now. Jason

and Shaun had been mistaken all their lives for brothers because of their similar looks.

Shaun. His best friend.

And Kara. Kara! The only woman he'd ever loved.

How was it possible his girl and his best friend had created a baby?

Pain spanned from temple to temple. This couldn't be happening. It had to be some kind of sick, twisted nightmare. Kara and Shaun never would have betrayed him like this.

Jason's breath came in short, rapid puffs.

"This can't be right. Kara, tell me it isn't true. Tell me you're saying this to get even with me for leaving you, and none of it is true."

"I can't."

"But how? Why?" The questions tumbled through his mind. "Did you always have a thing for him?"

"No. It was a mistake. A combination of too much to drink, a deep aching loneliness and hearing that Shaun loved me."

"He loved you?" Would the blows never stop coming?

"He admitted that he loved me, but up until then he hadn't been able to do anything about it, because of you...."

Jason ran a hand over his mouth, trying to remember some sign, some hint he'd missed. "I had no idea. How could I have been so blind?"

"You weren't the only one. I didn't know, either."

Her words didn't comfort him. Inside, he was mortally wounded, worse than when his father had smacked him in the face with the truth about his parentage. Jason had thought nothing could hurt worse than that, but he had been oh so wrong.

His vision grew blurry as he looked at Kara, no longer seeing the woman he loved, but rather the woman who'd betrayed him with his best friend, and stolen away the child he'd so wanted to be his little girl.

"Why?" His voice croaked out. "Why him?"

If it had been anyone else in the world, he'd have been able to deal with it. But not the one guy he'd considered a brother.

He had been wrong.

He couldn't forgive this.

If that made him less of a man, more a coward, so be it.

Shaun being the father of Kara's little girl made Jason's stomach lurch. The thought of his best friend and the woman he'd wanted to marry clinging to each other—Shaun's lips on hers—made the bile rush to the back of his mouth. Jason swallowed hard, pushing down the sickening thought.

When Kara opened her mouth to speak, he held up a hand to stop her. "Don't answer. I don't want to hear it. I can't believe you betrayed me with my best friend."

He couldn't stay here any longer. He was going to be ill.

In a few quick strides, barely noticing his injured knee's protest, he reached the door. His hand paused on the doorknob for just a moment. With a shake of his head to clear away the image of Kara in Shaun's arms, he yanked open the door and rushed into the frigid, dark night.

He'd never been so sick or so alone in his entire life.

CHAPTER FIFTEEN

HER PREDICTION HAD come true.

In this instance, Kara hated being right. But just as soon as Jason heard about her youthful mistake, he'd done exactly what she'd worried he would do...run. Of course, part of it was her fault. She'd waited too long to tell him about Shaun, and she hadn't prepared Jason at all. The whole situation couldn't have been handled any worse if she had tried.

Days had passed since that fateful night and Jason had completely avoided her, both in and out of the office. The devastation of him turning away like this made her anxious to find a new job. She'd let herself get in too deep with him. She'd let herself trust him, rely on him. In that instant, she realized how he'd sneaked past her best defenses.

She'd fallen in love with him.

She wasn't in love with the boy he used to be, the youth of her memories. No, she loved the man who'd saved her from a snowstorm and opened his home to her. The man who'd put her and Samantha's happiness above his own by taking time away from renovating the resort to decorate cookies and read a bedtime story.

What if Kara had told him she loved him? Would he have still walked out the door? Probably. He was unable to accept that she'd had a child with his best friend. The fact that their engagement had been officially dissolved at the time seemed completely immaterial to him.

But none of it mattered now. Whatever she'd thought they were building together was over and done. She had to focus on the new job she'd been offered in Ohio. It was in the next state, not that far from her family...or Jason, not that he'd ever visit them.

"Mommy, Mommy, look." Samantha hurried into the kitchen, holding a folded piece of red construction paper.

"What do you have there?"

"A Christmas card. See?" She held it two inches from Kara's face.

A step back allowed Kara's eyes to adjust and focus on the highly decorated paper. She noticed the green cutout of a Christmas tree and the shape of an angel at the top, reminiscent of the tree topper Jason had given them. Kara's bottom lip started to tremble at the thought of never having him drop by their house with little gifts for Samantha, or just to share a cup of hot cider and discuss his day with her.

"Do you like it?" Samantha asked, jarring Kara back to the present.

"It's lovely. You did a great job. But didn't we have a long talk about you not using the glue without asking?"

"Uh-huh. But it was a surprise."

"I understand, but don't do it again." She didn't have the heart to be more assertive. "You're quite the artist. I like how you used glitter to make the garland on the tree."

Her daughter ducked her head and shrugged. "I wanted it to look just like the tree Jason gave us."

Kara swallowed the lump that formed in her throat at the mention of his name. She had yet to tell Samantha that he wouldn't be coming to visit anymore. She knew it must be done sooner rather than later, but she also knew how attached her daughter was to him. How in the world was Kara supposed to break her heart?

"I have another picture I have to finish." Samantha turned and started out of the room.

"Wait," Kara called. "Don't you want me to put your card on the fridge?"

"Uh-uh. I made it for Jason."

Kara picked up the card and opened it. *"Merry Christmas, Jason. We miss you. XOXOXO Samantha."*

This was the moment she'd been dreading. Kara backed against the counter for support. "But honey, he's really busy with the resort. I don't know if he'll have time to visit again."

Samantha pressed her hands onto her hips. "Then you can give it to him at work."

"I'll try."

"You have to. Promise?"

Unable to deny helping her daughter with this gesture of kindness, Kara said, "I promise."

"Don't forget."

She wouldn't forget the card or Jason. Although she couldn't wait around for something that obviously wasn't meant to be. She'd been down this road before, but this time she knew she had to move on—to do what was best for her and Samantha. No matter how much it hurt.

Jason leaned back in his office chair late Thursday morning. He ran a hand through his hair, not caring if he messed it up. He didn't have any appointments, just a huge stack of mail, files to review and invoices to sign. He'd spent most of the week working on the lift on the double-diamond run. It'd taken three tries to get the right parts for such an old piece of equipment, but at last they'd done it. Things were finally on track for the grand reopening in two more days.

He'd spent months working toward this moment, and now that it was almost here, he should be excited, bursting with happiness. But without Kara and Samantha around to share his accomplishment, he was empty inside. They'd provided him with the driving force to overcome unforeseen problems and the strength to push through the long hours.

He picked up the phone to dial Kara's extension, but then slammed it back down. He had no idea what to say to her. Now that he'd had time to calm down and think everything through, he realized how poorly he'd reacted to her admission. What had he expected? For her to be a saint, and loyal, after the horrible way he'd ended their engagement and left town without even an explanation?

He had only himself to blame for everything that had happened. His heart pounded with unrelenting exasperation. How could he have handled this situation so horribly? Maybe he was more like the man who raised him than he'd ever imagined—unreliable. Jason found it strange how he found himself in such a similar position to the one his dad had been in years ago, both of them loving a woman who had a child by another man.

Jason's head hung low and shame washed over him at the way he'd failed while his father had succeeded. His dad had moved past the fact that Jason's mom was pregnant with another man's child. He'd married her and raised her baby as his own. Jason had to give the man credit; he'd tried to be a good father.

Jason shook his head. He hadn't even stepped up to the plate and welcomed the woman he loved and the daughter of his heart into his life. His hands clenched. Instead, he had lived up to Kara's worst nightmares and walked away from her. Again. She'd predicted that this was how he'd react when things got to be too much for him, and he'd proven her right.

There'd be no going back this time.

He ran his hands over his face. He'd really screwed up. Anger over his knee-jerk reaction balled up in his gut. After she'd forgiven him for leaving her, and accepted him, screwed-up genes and all, he'd overreacted to something she'd done years ago in a moment of confusion and pain.

A deep, guttural groan grew in the back of his throat. He'd ruined everything. His eyes closed as he tried to block it all out. Kara's image refused to fade away. The anguished look in her green eyes ripped at his gut. He clenched his hand and slammed it down on the desktop, making everything shake. The desk calendar fell over, a pen rolled off the edge and the stack of paperwork requiring his attention teetered over, spilling onto the floor.

With a frustrated sigh, he rose to his feet, surveying the mess of files and correspondence. He placed everything in a haphazard stack on his desk. Maybe some work would take his mind off the chaos he'd made of everyone's lives.

With a sigh, he sank down on his chair and tackled the very first item on the intimidating heap of paperwork. More than an hour later, he came across a plain white envelope. Jason looked at it and frowned when he found it still sealed. It was customary for his assistant to open everything and date stamp the correspondence. It wasn't like her to miss things.

He slipped a finger beneath the flap and yanked, ripping open the envelope. He pulled out a folded piece of red construction paper. When he saw the crude cutout of a Christmas tree, he was quite puzzled. He flipped it open and smiled at the scribbled, green crayon message, with Samantha's name printed across the bottom. He blinked repeatedly as he stared at the prettiest card he'd ever received.

Was it possible Kara didn't hate him? His hands began to shake as his hopes started to mount. Was this her attempt at a peace offering? Or had Samantha merely insisted she deliver the card? Either way, he was deeply touched by the gesture.

He set it on the desk and sucked in a deep, calming breath. He couldn't go off half-cocked—that was what had led him to this mess.

He glanced down. An old weathered envelope caught his attention. It was the letter from the man who'd hurt him so deeply—the same man who had taught him to fish and how to play ball. Jason stared at the envelope, remembering his promise to Kara to read it.

Maybe there really was such a thing as a Christmas miracle. Or maybe he needed to make a Christmas miracle of his own. He needed to prove to Kara that he had changed into a man she could trust with her heart, through the good and the bad. Words wouldn't be enough. He needed to do more. Perhaps this letter was the perfect place to start.

He ripped open the envelope, bracing himself for a string of hateful words. But when he read: *"Son, I'm sorry..."* his gaze blurred. He blinked repeatedly and kept reading the heartfelt note. His father hadn't meant what he'd said in his drunken rage. Jason checked the date, finding it'd been written almost seven years ago, while he was still in basic training. He'd wasted all these years being stubborn, thinking his dad hated him. But he'd been wrong.

Jason's throat grew thick with emotion. Kara had been right all along. This was the season for hope and forgiveness.

A plan started to take shape in his mind. He'd show her

that he could embrace the spirit of the season. He knew what must be done—the most important mission of his life. Operation: Win Kara Back.

And he didn't have a moment to lose. He'd already wasted seven years. He could be a reliable, steadfast man for Kara and a father to the little girl who'd already claimed a permanent spot in his heart. He wouldn't repeat his or his father's mistakes. He'd make sure both Kara and Samantha knew how much he loved them.

Jason shoved back from his desk. With long strides he headed for the office where Kara's desk stood. When he found her chair vacant, he spun around, scanning the shelving units, file cabinets and other desks. No Kara.

What if she'd quit? His chest tightened.

"Mr. Greene, do you need something?" asked Sherry, a redhead wearing a festive reindeer sweater.

"First, it's Jason, remember?"

She smiled, then nodded.

"Do you know where Kara is?" He'd track her down to the ends of the earth if that was what it took. He couldn't lose this chance to set things right. Something told him it would be the last chance he got.

"Oh, well…"

"Spit it out," he said, lacking any patience.

"I took a message for her when she stepped out to get some coffee. When I gave her the note, she grabbed her things, said she didn't know when she'd be back and ran out the door."

Had something happened to Samantha? Jason's heart lodged in his throat. But surely Kara would have said something. Then he realized, with the way he'd left things between them, he'd be lucky if she ever spoke to him again. And he couldn't blame her after the ass he'd made of himself.

"Do you remember the message?" he asked, praying for a little help here.

Sherry nodded. "It was the Pleasant Valley Care Home."

Regret sucker-punched him. His breath hitched. Kara's prediction had come true. Something had happened to his father and Jason had been too stubborn to go to him, to hear him out. Now it was too late to give his dad some peace of mind. Or was it? Was his guilty conscience jumping to conclusions?

"What did the message say?" he asked, poised to rush out the door.

"For her to come to the home—that Joe needed her."

Jason still had a chance to make things right.

He bolted toward the parking lot, hoping he wouldn't be too late to put his father's mind at ease. Jason might not have liked the drunk he had become, but the man he used to be, when Jason's mother was alive—he owed that man a bit of peace.

And Kara shouldn't be shouldering this all by herself. She might not want him there, but he owed it to her to at least make the attempt.

Jason clung to the hope that he wouldn't be too late as he tramped the accelerator on the way to the sprawling facility. He took the first available parking spot and ran to the door.

Out of breath, he said to a small group of women behind the counter, "I'm here to see my father."

One with bleach-blond hair and blue eye shadow directed him to sign in, gave him directions to the room and buzzed him through the double doors. Though the process took only a couple of minutes, each second dragged on forever.

The muscles in his shoulders and neck grew rigid as Jason strode down the wide corridor, checking each room number, his hands balled up at his sides. At last he reached room 115. He fully expected to see a flurry of nurses shouting out lifesaving orders, but instead the lilt of laughter echoed through the doorway. Kara was laughing?

He stood there in the hallway, breathing a sigh of relief. Little by little, his body began to relax. His father had to be okay or she wouldn't be laughing.

Suddenly he was caught up in a wave of second thoughts. Neither Kara nor his father knew he was standing just outside in the hallway. He could easily slip away and nobody would be the wiser. He'd be back...soon. Once he gave this reunion some thought and planned out what to say. Somehow "Hey, Dad, how's it going?" didn't quite work in this case.

His gaze swung back to the double doors leading toward the parking lot. It'd be so much easier, and he had so much work to do at the resort.

He'd stepped back when he heard someone say, "Mr. Greene, I see you found your father's room. You can go ahead in."

A pretty, young nurse with a brown ponytail was headed down the hall, carrying a white blanket. He vaguely remembered seeing her at the reception desk.

"Thanks."

More footsteps sounded and then Kara stood before him, her face lit up with a smile. In fact, he'd say she was glowing.

"I knew you'd eventually find your way here. In your own time."

His instinct was to deny he was here for any other reason than to check on her, but he couldn't. The time had come to be truthful about the feelings he'd been running from for too long. As crazy as it sounded, if there was a chance to see the man who'd called him son, Jason wanted to take it.

"They said at the office there was an emergency." He glanced into the room, but could only see the end of a bed and a couple of empty chairs.

"Everything is okay. Your father got worked up when a doctor he didn't know tried to examine him. His doc went out of town for the holidays and the newest associate drew the short straw, pulling holiday duty."

"You were able to sort it all out?"

She smiled and nodded.

Kara shouldn't be here, dealing with his father and the doctors. She had enough on her hands being a single mother. It was time he started shouldering the responsibilities where his father was concerned.

"Kara," a gruff voice called out, followed by a string of coughs.

"I'll be right there." She moved closer to Jason and lowered her voice. "Prepare yourself. He's a mere ghost of the man you left seven years ago."

Jason nodded, still not exactly sure what to expect. He couldn't imagine Joe as anything but six foot four, with shoulders like a linebacker and a stogie hanging out the side of his mouth.

"One more thing," she said. "If you came here to settle up on an old score—don't. He can't take the strain. He isn't strong enough."

Jason nodded once more.

"I mean it." Her tone left no uncertainty about her seriousness.

"I get it."

First, he'd deal with his dad, and then he'd talk to Kara. He started for the door, letting her follow him inside. His steps were slow but steady.

When at last he saw his father's face, he stopped. A word of greeting caught in his throat. He blinked, unable to imagine someone could physically change so drastically from a vibrant man to barely more than a skeleton with yellowing skin.

Jason choked down his alarm. The pitiful sight doused any lingering resentment inside him. There was nothing he could say to hurt this man any worse than he'd hurt himself. His father had suffered enough.

"Son, you came." A round of hacking coughs overtook him.

For a moment, Jason stood frozen, bombarded by his dad's appearance, from the oxygen tube aiding his breathing to the sunken eyes and the bony hand covering his mouth as he struggled through the fit of coughing. It was the distressed look on his father's face that finally kicked him into action. Jason stepped alongside the bed and filled a glass with water.

"Yes, Dad, I'm home."

After handing over the glass, Jason peered over his shoulder to make eye contact with Kara, but she was gone. Their talk would have to wait a little longer.

"I…I was worried." Joe paused to catch his breath. "Thought maybe I'd never lay eyes on you again."

"I'm here." He placed a reassuring hand on his father's bony shoulder. Jason schooled his features, hoping to keep his pity and shock under wraps. "Whatever you need, all you have to do is ask."

"You'd do that…now…after everything?" He coughed again.

"Yes."

The one syllable said enough. Jason didn't want to rehash the bad times, knowing they'd wasted too much time looking over their shoulders instead of appreciating the here and now. Besides, the letter had already told him everything he'd ever need to know. Too bad it'd taken him all these years to read it.

"Hey, Dad, remember those days when we'd head out with our fishing poles in hand to catch dinner?"

The corners of his father's thin lips lifted. "You remember back then?"

"I remember, Dad."

"We never did catch much."

"But it was fun trying."

"That it was." This time it was his father who reached out to him, squeezing his forearm with cool hands. "I was worried you'd forget those times." Another coughing fit overtook him and Jason offered him more water. When his breathing calmed, Joe continued, "I'm sorry it all went so wrong. I couldn't handle your mother's death, and I let you down."

Knowing this was no longer about him, but about giving his father everlasting peace, Jason added, "But before that you were the best dad. I wouldn't have made it to quarterback in high school if it hadn't been for you teaching me to play ball at an early age."

A twinkle came to his father's sunken eyes just before his eyelids began to droop. Obviously, the emotional reunion and the coughing had zapped his energy.

"It's okay, Dad. You rest now."

"Son, tell Kara I still want my Christmas present."

"I will." Jason hoped she knew what his father was talking about, because he certainly didn't. "I'll be back tomorrow to check on you."

"Promise?" Joe murmured. His eyes were completely closed now.

"I promise. You don't have to worry anymore. I'll be here when you need me."

And he knew without a doubt that he wasn't going any-where—no matter what fate threw at him. He would be here for the loved ones in his life. Now he just had to convince Kara to trust in him.

CHAPTER SIXTEEN

FRIDAY EVENING KARA'S heart hammered harder and faster the closer she got to Jason's log home. She could hardly believe he'd once again called and summoned her to drop everything, grab Samantha and come running.

This time he'd requested the vendor quotes. Of course, she couldn't blame him. She was supposed to have dropped the report on his desk on her way out the door, but a printer snafu and a phone call from her impatient daughter had left her thoughts scattered. Kara had walked right out the door with the printed report in hand.

But she also had some important information for him. After checking around with other restaurants, she knew what she didn't like about Bigger Wholesales—they undercut their competition with inferior produce, and a lot of money was lost due to waste.

As she made a left-hand turn onto Jason's road, she wondered if tonight might be a good time to let him know that she'd done a phone interview with the company in Ohio. Her background check had come back clean and now the only thing standing between her and an office manager position with benefits was for her to accept. She should be excited, or at least relieved, but she couldn't work up any enthusiasm for leaving her family, home or—most of all—Jason. It'd taken years to be reunited and now, in a blink, they were over.

A groan from behind had Kara glancing in the rearview mirror at her daughter, who was squirming in her seat belt. "Sweetie, what are you doing?"

"I dropped Bubbles." Guttural grunts sounded. "Got him."

"Maybe you should leave him in the car so you don't lose him while we're at Jason's. We won't be long."

"Bubbles stays with me."

Not in the mood for an argument, Kara let the subject drop. Jason's driveway loomed in the distance. A nervous energy made her stomach quiver at the thought of seeing him outside the office, where they didn't have to maintain a professional facade.

She glanced at the clock. Seven on the dot. They were right on time. She turned into the drive and was floored to find the entire house decked out in multicolored, twinkling Christmas lights. Her mouth gaped open.

"Mommy, look at all those lights."

"They're beautiful."

Tears threatened as she wondered if Jason's Scrooge-like view on life had at last changed. She quickly tamped down her emotions. It wasn't as if he'd done this for her. He must be planning to invite the investors to his house for a party or some such thing. He probably hated each and every one of the lights adorning his yard.

She glanced down at the gift she'd wrapped for him, wondering if perhaps she'd chosen the right thing to give him. Would he take offense? Still, she just couldn't run out and buy him any of the traditional gifts, such as a tie, flannel pajamas or a cheese tray. Those things didn't say "Jason" to her. But seeing the house all decked out with holiday fare reaffirmed her choice of gifts.

Her insides trembled as she pulled the car to a stop next to the porch. Before she had a chance to decide her next move, Santa stepped out onto the porch.

Santa?

"Mommy. Mommy, look."

When Santa moved in front of her headlights, and stared back at her through wire-rimmed glasses, Kara gaped again. Why in the world was the man she'd commonly thought of as Scrooge all dressed up like the jolliest man at the North Pole?

She swallowed hard, trying to comprehend what was going on here.

"Mommy, doesn't Jason look neat?" Samantha opened the door and scooted out of the backseat.

Too late to back out now.

He walked down the steps in his black boots and out the walk to greet them. Kara immediately noticed his lean waist had grown into a very plump tummy, with a thick black belt and a gold buckle holding everything in place.

"Ho-ho-ho." His deep voice rumbled.

"You make a good Santa," Samantha said, patting his rounded belly.

"And have you been naughty or nice?" he asked, in a Santa-like voice. "Ho-ho-ho."

Kara couldn't help but laugh. What in the world had gotten into him?

When she regained her composure, she asked, "Um… are we early?"

"You're right on time. You and Samantha are my only guests."

Her eyes opened wide. "You planned all this for us? What about the vendor report?"

"We'll go over it Monday at the office. Afraid that was just a ruse to get you here." He smiled sheepishly. "I know how much you enjoy the holidays and I thought you might appreciate the decorations. Do you like them?"

Samantha ran off to check out the various Christmassy figurines lining the porch, leaving the two adults with a little bit of privacy.

Kara gazed up into Jason's blue eyes and her world tilted off center. Giving a little tug on his cottony beard, she said, "I like Santa best of all."

"I'm so sorry, Kara. I was such a jerk the other night—"

"We've both done things we aren't proud of. I should have been totally straight with you from the beginning about what occurred after you left town."

His steady gaze held hers. "I wanted to show you just how much you both mean to me."

She bestowed upon him her biggest and brightest smile. "Well, Santa, you've outdone yourself. Especially today with your father. Thank you for making the effort."

"No, thank *you*. You finally talked some sense into me. It was way past time that my father and I patched things up. We'll never be candidates for a Norman Rockwell painting, but we've made peace with each other, and you won't have to worry about him so much anymore. I'll be there for him."

"I'm glad." She squeezed his arm.

"Let's go inside," he said, climbing the steps and opening the door for them.

When Kara stepped inside, Sly ran up to her with a loud meow, followed by a boisterous purr as she rubbed against her ankles. Kara bent down and ran her hand over the feline's satiny fur.

"Hey, sweetie. I missed you, too."

As though understanding Kara's words, Sly paused, lifted her golden eyes and meowed in agreement.

"Wow. A kitty." Samantha ran over and dropped to her knees.

Sly scampered away to a safe distance before turning and taking in the little girl with a cautious stare.

"Come here, Sly," Jason called to the cat.

Sly paused. Big, curious eyes checked them out before she sauntered over. In one fluid motion, Jason scooped up the cat in one arm and started to pet her.

"This is my friend Samantha," he said close to the cat's inky-black ear. "She's really nice." He leaned toward the little girl. "Go ahead and pet her head."

Kara smiled as Santa did his best to make her daughter feel at home. Her eyes glistened as she took in this tender moment. What in the world did all this mean? She didn't want to jump to conclusions. She was certain Jason would eventually explain.

In the background, she spotted the Christmas tree exactly as she'd left it. She couldn't stop smiling. Jason had let the joy of the holiday back into his heart. A happy tear splashed on her cheek. She swiped it away with the back of her hand.

Samantha ran over to the tree and sat on the floor next to it. The sleek feline followed, eventually rubbing against her arm.

"Look, Sly, at all the presents. There's three with my name on them." Samantha glanced over her shoulder at Jason. "Can I open them now?"

"Sure. If it's okay with your mom."

Kara nodded. As Samantha ripped into her gifts, Jason draped an arm over Kara's shoulders. "I hope I did okay. I've never bought toys for a little girl before. In fact, I've never bought toys before, period."

After Samantha unwrapped a pink plush cat, a jewelry

and makeup kit, and an electronic game, Kara said, "Samantha, don't we have a gift for Jason?"

Her daughter rushed over, removed a wrapped package from Kara's oversize purse and handed it to him. "It's your turn."

"What's this?" he asked, giving it a little shake.

Samantha shrugged.

"Just a little something," Kara stated.

He tore off the wrapping paper in much the same frenzied fashion as her daughter. "The angel." His brow crinkled. "But I gave this to Samantha."

Kara pressed a finger to his lips, stopping his protest. "This is a very precious gift, and Samantha and I enjoyed having her atop our tree. But it was time she came home where she belongs—with you." *The same place I want to be,* she almost added, but held her tongue. A heavy sadness settled in her heart as she blinked back the moisture gathering in her eyes.

Jason disappeared into the kitchen and returned with three champagne glasses. "Here's some sparkling cider. I thought it would fit the occasion." He handed each of them a glass and then held his high. "Here's to the two most wonderful ladies." He paused, clearing his throat. "May your futures be everything you want them to be."

Kara clinked her glass with his and forced a smile on her face. "And to a successful reopening."

She glanced up at him and saw the puzzled look in his eyes. He must have picked up something in her expression. Deep inside, she didn't want to move away. Living in a city meant there'd be no yard to plant spring flowers, and Samantha would have to go to an after-school day-care center while she worked, instead of staying with her doting grandparents. City life would be very different from what she'd imagined for her and Samantha.

And most of all, Jason wouldn't be around to drop by on a moment's notice. Oh, how she'd miss him, and the chance of them being more than just old friends. Sometimes life could be unfair.

Still, she couldn't discuss her reservations about the move. She had to maintain a positive front not only for Samantha but for herself. Kara stiffened her spine and swallowed down her misery. She'd wait until the day after Christmas to break the news of the move to her daughter. She didn't want to ruin the holiday.

CHAPTER SEVENTEEN

JASON TOOK KARA by the elbow and led her to the other side of the living room, giving them a little privacy.

"Will you give me another chance?" he asked, staring deep into her eyes.

"A chance for what?"

"For us. For you and me and Samantha to be together."

She continued to stare at him. Her eyes grew shiny but her lips didn't move.

"Kara." He placed a finger beneath her chin and lifted her head so their gazes met. "Talk to me. You want that, too, don't you?"

She blinked repeatedly while worrying her lower lip, as though internally waging a deep debate. Was it really so hard for her to decide? Was he about to lose her for good?

Jason searched her darkened eyes, detecting the swirl of confusion and utter frustration in them. "Please, say something."

"Why now?" Lines of stress creased her beautiful face. Her eyes pleaded with him to be honest. "If only you'd said something sooner, maybe we could have figured out something. But I've found a new job…in Ohio."

Her words sent his heart plummeting. He'd thought this through before she and Samantha had arrived. He knew there'd be hurdles to cross. Now wasn't the time to give up. If it meant he had to meet her halfway, or more than halfway, he'd do it.

"Come outside with me," he said, taking her arm.

"Outside?" She pulled back. "But why?"

"I need a few minutes to talk to you. Alone." He glanced over his shoulder at Samantha. "Don't worry, she'll be fine sitting next to the tree, with Sly by her side and her toys to occupy her."

"All right. Just for a couple of minutes."

He grabbed her coat from the back of the couch and draped it over her shoulders. After letting Samantha know where they'd be, Jason ushered Kara out the door into the chilly night.

A few inches of snow layered the ground and dusted the trees. With the lights he'd painstakingly strung over the porch rails and small trees and shrubs, it did look magical, if you were into that sort of thing. It wasn't something he'd normally have done; he considered it a labor of love. But as he stood here, looking out over the yard and watching colored lights twinkle on the snow, he had to admit it wasn't so bad.

"I still can't believe you put up all these decorations." Kara moved to his side.

When he turned his gaze back to the woman he loved—the woman he didn't want to let go for a second time—his insides twisted with anxiety. He'd never been so nervous about anything in his life, not even making his way through boot camp or being sent into enemy territory.

"I saw the worried expression on your face when I made the toast," he said. "Is there a problem with your new job?"

She shook her head. "No. Not at all. In fact, they're anxious for me to get settled into my new position."

Not what he wanted to hear, but nothing he couldn't handle. "So you're going ahead with the move?"

"Of course. Why wouldn't I? This is an amazing opportunity."

"I'm sure it is." Jason swallowed back his disappointment.

"You know, it's beautiful here," she said, leaning her hands on the rail. "You're so lucky to have this little piece of nature."

He turned to her and she stared up at him. The gentle breeze carried with it the scent of strawberries from her golden hair. The nippy air also brought out the pink hue in her smooth cheeks. And the red of her lips intensified, drawing his full attention to them. They looked so perfect for kissing.

"*Beautiful* doesn't even begin to describe it," he murmured, never moving his gaze from her.

"The yard looks amazing with all the lights. Did you do all this for us?"

He nodded. "If it's what makes you happy, then it's what makes me happy."

"And that Santa suit… You really outdid yourself." Her gaze slid over him, and he grew self-conscious when she eyed the puffy pillow widening his midsection.

"I need to apologize for being such a jerk the other night. Seven years ago, I dumped you. You were free to do whatever you wanted with your life. And I've accepted that. I'm sorry I overreacted. Most of all, I'm sorry I put you in that position all those years ago."

Her fingers reached out and touched his cheek. "We may have not made the best decisions back then, but despite them something miraculous happened. I gave birth to the most wonderful little girl." Kara turned to the living room window and he followed suit, glancing in at Samantha. "I've never for one instance regretted her."

"Nor do I," he admitted, surprised by his own heartfelt

sincerity. "She may not have my DNA, which is probably a blessing in itself—"

Kara elbowed him. "We had this conversation already, remember? You were created from your mother's love and Joe's best intentions. A child would be fortunate to have you as their father."

Her confidence in him warmed his insides. How could he have ever doubted her and her ability to handle his secret?

"Do you really mean that?"

"Of course I do."

"Santa almost forgot. He has one more gift to hand out." He reached beneath his costume and fished out a small box wrapped in red foil and tied up tight with a bow. He held it out to her. "Here. Open it."

Her eyes grew round. Her searching gaze moved from him to the tiny present.

"Go ahead," he coaxed. "It won't bite. I promise."

Her fingers trembled as she pulled on the ribbon, but they were no match for the quivering in his stomach. The most important mission of his life had finally reached the critical juncture. He had to succeed with this part of his plan. Otherwise his heart would end up a fallen victim on the front line.

Kara deftly made her way past the wrapping to the black velvet box. As though she was afraid to stop, she quickly lifted the lid.

Her lips formed an O.

Unspoken questions filled her eyes. She stood there staring at him like a deer caught in headlights, not knowing which way to go. She didn't throw the box at him and stomp away. Nor did she squeal with delight and throw herself in his arms. He'd take her reserve as a positive sign.

He still had time to convince her that they could make this thing between them work. He *had* to convince her.

"Don't say anything," he said, pressing a finger to those delectable lips. "Just listen. We can make this work."

She shook her head, her eyes shimmering. He fortified his determination with the knowledge that she hadn't heard his proposal yet. Once she did, she'd realize the possibilities for them.

"First, I love you," he said, gazing straight into her eyes. "I've always loved you. I am so sorry for destroying our dreams all those years ago. I wasn't mature enough back then to have faith in you and me—in us—to handle the news about my biological father."

Jason reached out and took her free hand in his. He rubbed his thumb over her cold fingers. He had to speed this up so he could get her back inside, next to the fire.

"I know how important this new job is to you. I can't expect you to change your plans and drop everything to live here in the country with me."

"What are you saying?"

"I'll move with you. You, me and Samantha will be a family."

"You'll move." Disbelief rang in her voice. "But you can't! You've only just come back. Your father needs you. And you're about to reopen the resort."

He'd done some serious thinking about this and he knew what he had to do. "I'll have my father transferred to wherever we are, and I'll sell the resort."

"Sell the resort?" Her brows arched. "You can't!" she repeated. "You just restored it."

He swallowed the jagged lump in his throat. "The Summit is important to me, but not as important as you and Samantha. I can be with the two of you and lose the resort and still be happy. But having the resort without the two most important people in my life would be a hollow victory."

Kara pressed a hand to her chest. "You really mean that, don't you?"

He nodded. "I'll do whatever it takes for us to be a family. I love you more than ever. And Samantha. She may not be my biological daughter, but she's the daughter of my heart."

"Oh, Jason. I love you, too. But I can't let you do this."

He took both Kara's hands in his. "Yes, you can. I was the one who walked out on our plans seven years ago. It's only fair that I fit into the life you've created for yourself, no matter where it is."

"The thing is, I don't want to move. I want to stay right here with you, my family and friends." She stepped into his open arms, resting her head beneath his chin. "Do you really think we can make it work?"

"I do. I've changed. I've grown up. With honesty between us, we can face anything."

She looked up at him, their breath intermingling. He couldn't resist his desire to taste her sweetness. His head dipped low. His lips met hers. She was compliant and eager beneath him. A moan rose in the back of his throat. He'd never, ever grow tired of kissing her.

As much as he hated to pull back from her, they needed to finish this conversation. They still had one more thing to discuss.

"It's starting to snow," he said, remembering the last time they'd been here and it had snowed—the miraculous night when she'd made him feel love again.

She turned, leaning back against his chest as they both watched fat snowflakes drifting down. "Do you think we'll get stuck here?"

He pulled her close. "One can only hope. By the way,

my dad said to tell you he's waiting for his Christmas present. Mind explaining?"

She laughed. The sound was the most delightful he'd ever heard. "Your father won't let me forget. I promised to knit him a red scarf so he can wear it outside. He misses the snow. He wants to feel it on his face once more."

"Is the scarf done?"

She nodded.

"Looks like if this snow keeps up we'll have a Christmas wish to fulfill."

"It'll be a Christmas of miracles."

Now was the perfect moment for the last thing he had to ask her. He dropped to his knee. "Kara Jameson, I've loved you since we were kids, and you mean more to me with each passing day. Please tell me that you'll be my best friend, my lover and my wife." He took the ring from the box and held it out to her. "Say you'll be Mrs. Jason Greene."

Tears dripped onto her pink cheeks. "Yes. Yes! *Yes!*"

His heart felt as if it would burst with joy. He slipped the ring onto her finger, stood up and pulled her into his arms, then swooped in and planted a gentle kiss on her lips. Her arms slipped up around his neck. He'd never felt this deeply for someone in his life.

"I saw Mommy kissing Santa Claus…." They turned to find Samantha grinning at them, happiness twinkling in her eyes. "Does this mean I get the present I really want for Christmas?"

Kara's eyes met her daughter's. Unable to contain her joy, she smiled back. "What present is that?"

"I want Jason to live with us. He can be my daddy."

Jason smiled, and Kara draped her arm around his waist and leaned into him. "I think that can be arranged," she said.

He knelt on one knee again and held out his arms. Samantha rushed into them. "I'd be honored to be your father."

Over her head, Jason's gaze met Kara's. "I can't think of anything I'd love more than to be part of this wonderful family."

* * * * *

Mills & Boon® Hardback

October 2013

ROMANCE

The Greek's Marriage Bargain	Sharon Kendrick
An Enticing Debt to Pay	Annie West
The Playboy of Puerto Banús	Carol Marinelli
Marriage Made of Secrets	Maya Blake
Never Underestimate a Caffarelli	Melanie Milburne
The Divorce Party	Jennifer Hayward
A Hint of Scandal	Tara Pammi
A Façade to Shatter	Lynn Raye Harris
Whose Bed Is It Anyway?	Natalie Anderson
Last Groom Standing	Kimberly Lang
Single Dad's Christmas Miracle	Susan Meier
Snowbound with the Soldier	Jennifer Faye
The Redemption of Rico D'Angelo	Michelle Douglas
The Christmas Baby Surprise	Shirley Jump
Backstage with Her Ex	Louisa George
Blame It on the Champagne	Nina Harrington
Christmas Magic in Heatherdale	Abigail Gordon
The Motherhood Mix-Up	Jennifer Taylor

MEDICAL

Gold Coast Angels: A Doctor's Redemption	Marion Lennox
Gold Coast Angels: Two Tiny Heartbeats	Fiona McArthur
The Secret Between Them	Lucy Clark
Craving Her Rough Diamond Doc	Amalie Berlin

Mills & Boon® Large Print

October 2013

ROMANCE

The Sheikh's Prize	Lynne Graham
Forgiven but not Forgotten?	Abby Green
His Final Bargain	Melanie Milburne
A Throne for the Taking	Kate Walker
Diamond in the Desert	Susan Stephens
A Greek Escape	Elizabeth Power
Princess in the Iron Mask	Victoria Parker
The Man Behind the Pinstripes	Melissa McClone
Falling for the Rebel Falcon	Lucy Gordon
Too Close for Comfort	Heidi Rice
The First Crush Is the Deepest	Nina Harrington

HISTORICAL

Reforming the Viscount	Annie Burrows
A Reputation for Notoriety	Diane Gaston
The Substitute Countess	Lyn Stone
The Sword Dancer	Jeannie Lin
His Lady of Castlemora	Joanna Fulford

MEDICAL

NYC Angels: Unmasking Dr Serious	Laura Iding
NYC Angels: The Wallflower's Secret	Susan Carlisle
Cinderella of Harley Street	Anne Fraser
You, Me and a Family	Sue MacKay
Their Most Forbidden Fling	Melanie Milburne
The Last Doctor She Should Ever Date	Louisa George

ROMANCE

Million Dollar Christmas Proposal	Lucy Monroe
A Dangerous Solace	Lucy Ellis
The Consequences of That Night	Jennie Lucas
Secrets of a Powerful Man	Chantelle Shaw
Never Gamble with a Caffarelli	Melanie Milburne
Visconti's Forgotten Heir	Elizabeth Power
A Touch of Temptation	Tara Pammi
A Scandal in the Headlines	Caitlin Crews
What the Bride Didn't Know	Kelly Hunter
Mistletoe Not Required	Anne Oliver
Proposal at the Lazy S Ranch	Patricia Thayer
A Little Bit of Holiday Magic	Melissa McClone
A Cadence Creek Christmas	Donna Alward
Marry Me under the Mistletoe	Rebecca Winters
His Until Midnight	Nikki Logan
The One She Was Warned About	Shoma Narayanan
Her Firefighter Under the Mistletoe	Scarlet Wilson
Christmas Eve Delivery	Connie Cox

MEDICAL

Gold Coast Angels: Bundle of Trouble	Fiona Lowe
Gold Coast Angels: How to Resist Temptation	Amy Andrews
Snowbound with Dr Delectable	Susan Carlisle
Her Real Family Christmas	Kate Hardy

ROMANCE

His Most Exquisite Conquest	Emma Darcy
One Night Heir	Lucy Monroe
His Brand of Passion	Kate Hewitt
The Return of Her Past	Lindsay Armstrong
The Couple who Fooled the World	Maisey Yates
Proof of Their Sin	Dani Collins
In Petrakis's Power	Maggie Cox
A Cowboy To Come Home To	Donna Alward
How to Melt a Frozen Heart	Cara Colter
The Cattleman's Ready-Made Family	Michelle Douglas
What the Paparazzi Didn't See	Nicola Marsh

HISTORICAL

Mistress to the Marquis	Margaret McPhee
A Lady Risks All	Bronwyn Scott
Her Highland Protector	Ann Lethbridge
Lady Isobel's Champion	Carol Townend
No Role for a Gentleman	Gail Whitiker

MEDICAL

NYC Angels: Flirting with Danger	Tina Beckett
NYC Angels: Tempting Nurse Scarlet	Wendy S. Marcus
One Life Changing Moment	Lucy Clark
P.S. You're a Daddy!	Dianne Drake
Return of the Rebel Doctor	Joanna Neil
One Baby Step at a Time	Meredith Webber